# THE BUTTERFLY GAME

Gloria Davidson Marlow

Second Printing, 2014
Printed in the United States of America

Published By Salt Run Publishing LLC

http://saltrunpublishing.com

ISBN-13: 978-1-62390-018-2

# Contents

# CHAPTER ONE

Central Florida

*Standing in the shadow of the huge live oak, he watched the girl who would be his next victim. She was perfect, absolutely perfect. His breathing quickened with anticipation as he caught sight of the van parked across the field with its logo sparkling in the sunlight. Butterfly Cosmetics. What clearer sign could he ask for?*

*The girl's laughter caught his attention and he leaned forward excitedly as an even clearer, more miraculous sign proving she was the one met his eyes.*

Genevieve Lewiston laughed as the box at her feet was opened and the butterflies flew up toward her, their wings barely brushing her skin. For a moment, they fluttered toward her, and then quickly dispersed into the clear, blue sky overhead. She looked toward Evan Cowart, the director, who opened his mouth to speak, but remained silent as he stared at her shoulder in slack-jawed surprise. Her eyes followed his and she smiled at the large black and red butterfly perching on the strap of her white sundress. They studied each other for a minute before the butterfly lifted off to join its fellows and Genevieve turned toward Evan Cowart, turquoise eyes sparkling with joy.

"My God," he breathed. "Did you get that?"

The cameraman, Jeff Larson, nodded as Evan shot the question at him.

"That was perfect, Gen. Cannon's going to love it."

He was already dialing Cannon Brockway's number on his mobile phone as she walked away and she grinned as he heard him pronouncing the moment "magical."

Cannon, the owner of Butterfly Cosmetics would be overjoyed with the way the commercial had turned out. Once at the van, -

1

Genevieve found an empty lawn chair and leaned back. She studied her surroundings as she basked in the Florida sunshine. Even in spring, the heat could be brutal in Florida. Today, it was tempered by a soft breeze wafting through the leaves of the trees, which formed a semi-circle around the meadow. She lifted her hand in greeting at the teenage boy slumped against a tree across the field. Even from this distance she could see his face turn a fiery red as he darted away.

Jeff chuckled as he opened the van doors.

"Poor kid. He's been standing there for hours thinking we didn't see him. Now you've gone and scared him away."

Her eyes shot to where the boy had been standing. It seemed she'd always had that affect on boys. Since her first appearance in an ad for Butterfly Cosmetics, she hadn't been able to form a serious relationship. Whom was she kidding? She hadn't been able to form any sort of relationship, serious or otherwise. She had been sixteen the first time she appeared on a commercial. She had just gotten her first serious crush on a boy when she was rushed from a bespectacled bookworm to the cover girl for the most popular cosmetic line in the South.

"So are you going to the party with Patty tonight or are you staying home and studying again?" Jeff asked, interrupting her reverie as he packed the equipment into the back of the van.

Genevieve started to tell him she was staying home, but in a moment of uncharacteristic spontaneity, she nodded.

"Yeah, I think I will go. It's been forever since I went to a party and Suzy will enjoy it."

"It's been forever since you went anywhere," Evan's assistant, Richard, said as he came up behind Jeff with another dolly loaded with equipment. His perpetual scowl diminished a little at the mention of her friend, Suzy's, name. "Suzy will be ecstatic."

"Speaking of ecstatic," Jeff nodded his head toward the spot where Evan still stood waving his hands about as if the person on the other end of the phone could see the motions.

"Was it that good?" Genevieve asked looking toward the two men for an honest answer. Jeff was a terrible liar and Richard was

2

brutally honest, so they were the two people whose opinion she sought after every shoot.

"It was the perfect moment," Jeff said and she caught the dreamy, almost awed quality of his voice.

Jeffery was the artist of the crew. Between him and Evan, they had created some truly wonderful ads, both for magazines and television.

Genevieve turned to Richard, expecting some sort of negative comment from him. Richard was a pessimist through and through, but he was truthful and that was what she wanted at this moment.

"If Cannon wanted a sign that this was the way we should go with the ad campaign, I think he got it," Richard said.

Cannon Brockway watched the girl on the screen turn her face toward the butterfly; the auburn locks of her hair framing her face as she stared at the beautiful creature.

As the butterfly flew away, Genevieve turned toward the camera with a quick smile that wrinkled her nose in that totally unconscious gesture that had endeared her to millions and her unusual turquoise eyes met the camera head on. Evan froze the image on the screen and Cannon caught his breath.

Coral lipstick, light blush, just a touch of brown eye shadow, all brought out the natural beauty of her face. That was how mothers and fathers wanted their daughters to look, beautiful, but natural. Like a butterfly.

The film rewound to the moment before the butterfly took flight. A deep, masculine voice gave the voice-over.

"Magical moments, like beauty, come naturally with Butterfly Cosmetics."

The slogan ended with Genevieve's smile.

Cannon let out his breath as Evan shut off the film. The silence grew heavy around them as Evan sat nervously on the seat across the conference table from him.

"Well?" he prodded when the silence got the best of him.

"I'm speechless," Cannon said running his fingers through his blond hair. "Totally speechless. That was the best I've seen her yet."

"She is the best thing we've ever done," Evan said with a nod. "Where is she anyway?"

Evan looked at Cannon disapprovingly, but Cannon dismissed his glare with a wave. It was the usual way of things when Cannon's semi-obsession with Genevieve became obvious. Evan disapproved and Cannon dismissed him. Still, Evan tried. She was a special girl, and he didn't want to see her hurt like all the girls before her.

"For Pete's sake, Evan. I just like to keep her close. She's a pleasure just to have in the same room. And she's my most valuable possession. She helped make Butterfly Cosmetics what it is today."

"She's at a party with Suzy Wiggins and Patty Hanover."

"Call her and tell her to come down. Believe me, she'll welcome the excuse. She hates parties."

"You are gorgeous," Cannon whispered as the commercial faded out.

Genevieve shifted uncomfortably in her seat. Cannon always made her nervous when he got that intense look in his eyes, the vivid blue irises darkening as they ran over her face and form. So far he had never made a move on her, but she was beginning to hear the clock ticking down on the day he would.

"Evan has impeccable vision," she said as she stood and pulled the purse strap over her shoulder. "It's a beautiful commercial."

At twenty-two, she was probably a little too old to feel this uncomfortable about being alone with a man who was so obviously attracted to her. Especially one as handsome as Cannon Brockway, the typical California surfer type with blond hair that was a tad too long, sun-bronzed skin and a body that was testament to the hours he spent in the gym every night. Most girls would give their right arm to have him look at them like he was looking at her, but she had been regaled with too many stories about the consummate playboy's exploits. She had no intention of becoming his next conquest.

He was beside her before she reached the door, his hand closing over her upper arm, before gently caressing its way down

4

her forearm to close around her wrist. His desire was clearly written on his face and she tried to pull away.

"Stay, Genevieve," he said softly as he tried to pull her closer.

She shook her head and opened the door a crack.

"Please," he asked, his thumb rubbing the sensitive skin of her wrist. "Let me make love to you."

"Cannon, if you want me to keep working for you any length of time after tonight, don't do this," she warned quietly.

He stared hard at her for a moment, as if trying to garner the sincerity behind her threat. She felt relief rush through her as he sighed and dropped her arm.

"Sorry," he mumbled looking for a moment like a little boy caught with his hand in the cookie jar.

"Don't let it happen again," she admonished, slipping out the door. "Good night, Cannon."

She could feel his eyes on her as she walked down the hall, but she stepped into the elevator without looking back and breathed a sigh of relief when the doors shut behind her.

Tonight was the closest Cannon had ever come to trying to seduce her and she was afraid it would change their relationship for the worse. Not because he would be angry, but because she felt as if a line had been crossed between them and their whole relationship could be affected by it.

If only Evan had stayed in the room, Cannon would have kept his feelings to himself. But when Cannon swept her up in an exuberant greeting upon her arrival, Evan stormed out of the room and hadn't reappeared. So, Cannon had crossed a line and now here she was, wondering if she should tell him her decision to quit modeling sooner rather than later.

He would be devastated. Not because of her personally. She knew better than to think that his pursuit of her was anything but a momentary diversion for him. He would be devastated because he would have to start all over again with another advertising campaign. But he would have had to someday anyway, and surely the thought had entered his mind that this might be drawing to a close when she graduated from college next month.

She exited the elevator and walked through the lobby. There was a pizza restaurant on the next block and she intended to consume a few pieces before curling up in her room with a good book.

As she stepped out onto the sidewalk, she remembered Cannon's fury when she told him she was majoring in education.

Evan on the other hand, had encouraged her to wash her hands of Cannon Brockway and the modeling world before they washed theirs of her. She knew she could become yesterday's face in a flash and it would all be over. Lately, she just wished it would hurry up and happen. Except for days like today, she corrected herself. It had been a magical moment when the butterfly had perched on her shoulder. The whole experience had been surreal. As the flutter of them had brushed past her on their way to the sky, she'd loved it. She smiled now as she thought of the gently kiss of their wings on her face.

She didn't hear the man slip up behind her, nor did she have a moment to fight him as he wrapped his arm around her from behind and covered her face with the chloroform-soaked rag.

# CHAPTER TWO

*He watched her as she slept, the beautiful redhead with eyes the color of the Caribbean Sea. With trembling hands, he touched her skin softly. Delicate but earthy, like the brown and orange butterfly he placed on her chest. Junonia genoveva.*

*Every morning until the day she died, he watched Vanessa apply the same soft color to her lips that Genevieve Lewiston wore. Sitting at her vanity table, she was the prettiest girl he'd ever seen. The thought of her smile when he told her she was the real Butterfly Girl brought tears to his eyes.*

*Leaning closer to Genevieve Lewiston, he breathed deeply of the soft scent of the perfume created by Butterfly Cosmetics. With a small wistful smile, he slowly wrapped the plastic around her. Once she was safely tucked away in her cocoon, he sat back on his heels and closed his eyes.*

*Again, his mind was filled with memories of Vanessa as she had been, laughing as they had sped down the back roads of Florida. She pointed out butterflies as they drove, as they picnicked, as they simply lay back and relaxed on the woven blanket she kept in the trunk of the car. Most of the butterfly names she knew by heart. The ones she didn't, she quickly found and circled in the well-worn butterfly book she carried with her everywhere.*

*Even after she became ill, she kept the book close. He'd put her bed close by the huge picture window in the living room of the house they shared. From there, she could watch as the butterflies flocked to the flower garden she'd planted the year she married him.*

*A single tear tracked its way down his cheek and fell onto the book that was opened in his lap as he knelt beside Genevieve.*

*He thought of how Genevieve had looked standing in the field today and the very moment the butterfly had landed on her*

7

*shoulder. He had known Vanessa's butterfly, the Vanessa atalanta, on sight. As soon as he'd seen it escape the confines of the box at Genevieve's feet, he had known it was Vanessa's. He'd been amazed when she had perched there on Genevieve's shoulder.*

*It had been a sign. Vanessa approved of what he was doing. She liked that he was playing her game.*

# CHAPTER THREE

St. Augustine, Florida
Six years later

Jenny Lewis hurried down the narrow street that lead away from the bustle of Saint George Street to the relative quiet of the bed and breakfast district a few blocks away.

She fought the urge to look over her shoulder, telling herself there was no one there. No one was following behind her. No one was bent on doing her harm.

Her breath hitched in her throat as she rushed up the wooden steps into the small two-story house that was hers and slammed the door shut behind her. Leaning weakly against the doorframe, she thanked God for seeing her safely home and faced the painful knowledge that the fear was back. She supposed if she were to be totally truthful with herself, she would admit the fear was always there, every season, every day, but springtime was the worst. It was always as the sky turned the beautiful cerulean blue of spring and the dogwoods began to bloom, that the fear increased until it was nearly debilitating.

Sometimes as the nights grew shorter and the whippoorwills began to call, she thought she could feel him near her, waiting silently, like a frog waiting for a fly.

She would never forget the bright spring day that had changed her life forever. It had been such a beautiful day. It was the kind of day that had earned Florida its nickname: the Sunshine State, all orange groves and seashells. It was a day that quite effectively hid the evil that stalked her, a day that gave no hint of the nightmare her life would become.

She could still remember waking to the feel of the heavy plastic pressing into her face, the panic when she realized her hands and feet were bound. She had moved her head back and forth,

9

crying out against her cruel confinement, but to no avail. She couldn't escape the plastic shroud he had wrapped her in before dumping her unconscious body on the banks of the Indian River.

Some small part of her panicked mind came to realize she could feel the smallest hint of a breeze on her cheek and she wasn't completely out of air. It took valiant effort to calm her mind and think rationally, but she had managed to work the plastic with her head until the opening had become big enough to let in an adequate amount of air.

She had no idea how long she had been there as she watched the sun rise, set and rise again. As the sun beat down on her burning body, she had accepted the fact that she would die there in her cocoon, with no one but the gulls who were gathering nearby for company.

She was barely alive when a fisherman found her there. She had lived, but had never been the same. She had quit her job with Butterfly Cosmetics and become a teacher. She had found a home on a quiet street in St. Augustine within walking distance of the eclectic mixture of shops and history that made up the old town. With its tiny yard and stone fence covered in wisteria, the century old wooden house had been a perfect place for her to become Jenny Lewis, a quiet unassuming schoolteacher no one would ever link to the Butterfly Girl.

She had a few close friends, a number of acquaintances and an ever-changing array of strangers who visited the historical city she adored; the city that seemed a world away from the river in Brevard County where she had been left for dead.

It had been almost six years since that day and still, as spring became summer, she felt the heavy weight of fear coiled inside her like a huge black snake, waiting for him to find her.

*He ran his fingers across the wings of the black butterfly, tracing the red spots with his fingertips.*

*"Vanessa," he whispered her name as the scent wafting from the open perfume bottle on the table brought the memories cascading around him.*

*He wasn't sure anymore when it had begun: this crazy obsession with the game his wife had played. He thought it had started sometime during the first year she was gone. He couldn't remember the exact day he had known what he needed to do, but he remembered the moment like it was just yesterday instead of nearly ten years ago.*

*They were married a year when she became ill and he watched as the beautiful girl he loved withered and vanished right before his eyes. He tried to hold onto her, tried to make her stay, but she simply smiled that sad, sweet smile that was hers alone and faded away.*

*She died here in this room, as he held her on his lap in the overstuffed chair she bought from an estate sale. It was a hideous chair embroidered with mauve butterflies, but she declared it perfect for her butterfly room. He never dreamed he would sit holding her in his arms as she slipped out of his life and into heaven.*

*He held her for hours, as butterflies of myriad color, shape and size stared out at him and grief overwhelmed him. Her voice grew weaker and weaker as she told him all she knew of the butterflies, the scientific names and the popular names, their habitats and the trivial little facts only she cared to know.*

*Scalding tears dripped down his cheek as spoke. He'd heard it all before, been tutored on all the facts, but he listened carefully, knowing it would be the last time he ever heard the delight in her voice as she spoke.*

*"I received my specimen of the vanessa atalanta, the Red Admiral Butterfly. See, I pinned her right there in the middle." She pointed weakly to the huge display case with its blue velvet spreading board. "She looks lonesome there all by herself, doesn't she? I always planned to collect all the butterflies that had women's names. I had the case made especially for them. Most people don't know how many butterflies share women's names, but there are quite a few of them. Like the vanessa, no one knows that's her name."*

*She was quiet for a moment and he sat holding her, his grief thick in his throat.*

11

*"I have this silly little game I play, sometimes," she said into the silence. "When I hear someone call a woman by name and I know that it's the name of a butterfly, I try to match something about her to the butterfly. Most of the time, the woman and the butterfly have nothing in common, but sometimes, they do. Maybe it's the color of her eyes or her hair, or the way she moves."*

*She grew silent then, and he knew the time had come to speak their last tender good-byes. As death beckoned, she looked up at him with eyes that glowed with unearthly light and whispered the words that were to haunt him forever.*

*"I hope there are butterflies in heaven."*

# CHAPTER FOUR

Outside her classroom window, Jenny could see the track where two of her favorite students ran side by side. They waved at someone standing nearby and Jenny's heart beat a little faster at the sight of the coach, Nick Jensen.

He really was one of the best looking men she had ever seen. The sun glinted off his dark brown hair, casting it with lighter, golden highlights as he nodded at the kids and turned back toward the gym. He moved with fluid, athletic grace, his long legs eating up the ground between the track and the gym. When he disappeared inside, she sighed quietly and turned away from the window.

"Hi, Jen," Anne Davis, the eleventh grade English teacher, said from the doorway.

"Hi, Anne. Come in." Jenny smiled and waved a hand in the direction of the chair in front of her desk.

"He's a really nice looking guy, huh?" Anne said with a grin.

"Who?" Jenny asked, hoping she sounded convincing.

"Nick Jensen," Anne looked at her sternly. "Don't try to play dumb with me. I saw you were checking him out when I came to the door. Not that I blame you. I was doing the same thing."

Jenny caught the teasing note in Anne's voice and felt the blush that stole across her cheeks.

"No sense being embarrassed, Jen. There isn't one of us who hasn't checked him out. There are a few who have even asked him out. He turns everyone down. I figure he must still be in love with his ex-wife."

"Why do you think that?" Jenny asked.

"Because he's definitely not gay, if you know what I mean. And no normal man that looks that good would spend every night alone unless he's in love."

"Oh," Jenny nodded her head, trying to make sense of the logic of Anne's statement.

"Well, I guess I'd better go." Anne stood up, still peering out the window as she backed out of the door.

Jenny glanced outside and saw Nick striding from the gym to the parking lot beyond.

"See ya," Anne called as she rushed from the room, giving Jenny the impression she was preparing to sprint down the stairs so she could catch Nick before he made it to his pickup truck.

*Poor Nick,* she thought with a grimace. *Does he even know he's being hunted?*

He had been the talk of the school since the day he started working here last year, and he figured into many fantasies whispered about in the teacher's lounge. There was no shortage of women throwing themselves at him daily, and it had come as a shock to her as well everyone else when he asked her out his second week here.

She was sure she had looked at him as if he were insane before politely but firmly refusing his offer. When she thought about it, she still felt as stunned as she had then. No one had asked her out in years, and she couldn't figure out why anyone as good-looking and personable as Nick Jensen would want to go out with her anyway. He must have tons of beautiful single women at his beck and call, so why he had singled her out was a mystery it was best not to explore.

He had never asked her out again, but didn't appear to hold her refusal against her. Just as they had before his invitation, they still enjoyed some very pleasant and interesting conversations in the teachers' lounge. Although she had little to say about her own past, she loved listening to him recounting his adventures with his rather large, close knit family. Whether his anecdotes were from years past or last weekend, he always made her laugh at some point in the story, and they had fallen into an easy friendship. In the back of her mind, she knew exactly how easy it would be for her to let more happen between them. But she had decided years ago that a quasi-relationship wasn't enough for her, and a real relationship would cost too much. It would force her to open herself up and spill her

14

secrets, and she couldn't do that right now, maybe not ever. She could never let them know who she had been or what had happened to her for fear the man who had tried to kill her would return for her. Something told her any relationship she had with Nick Jensen would be all or nothing, and since she wasn't willing to give all, she had to make do with nothing.

"Honey, I'm home," Jenny called as she pushed the kitchen door open.

Milton padded into the kitchen, a blue leash dangling from his mouth and a hopeful look in his eyes. She squatted down beside the huge Chesapeake Bay retriever she'd adopted three years ago, chuckling as she clipped the leash to his collar.

"I know, I know. It was a long day to be cooped up here all alone, wasn't it?" His tail thumped happily in response and she patted his red coat lovingly.

The unwelcome tug of fear reared its ugly head as she stood on the porch searching the dusk for shadow or substance. No matter how many times she stepped outside for their evening walk, she did the same thing, not even knowing what she searched for, only knowing she must search. She had to be sure whomever or whatever she feared wasn't waiting to pounce on her in the dark. She hated the fear that still lived inside her, the power that it had over her, and she hated the faceless assailant who had caused it. Anger and frustration at herself for letting him ruin even a moment of her life rushed through her. Taking a deep breath to fortify herself, she stepped into the approaching darkness.

She stalked down the block with Milton, who ordinarily led the way, trailing behind her. When they reached the empty, moonlit playground, he whined a little. His eyes searched the swings and jungle gym for the children who were there earlier in the day.

"Come on, Milton," she said, and as if he recognized her mood, he followed obediently. He gave her a soft bark of reproach as she led him past the duck pond without stopping to let him sniff the water's edge.

She glanced over her shoulder at him, stopping when she saw how downcast he looked with his head and tail dragging and golden eyes glancing longingly toward the water.

15

"Fine," she said, bending to unclip his leash. "Go find them. I'll wait for you here."

The dog growled a low warning deep in his throat at the same instant that Jenny became aware of the man standing behind her. She swallowed hard and said a quick prayer for courage and protection as she prepared to sprint away from him if need be.

"Jenny?"

The familiar sound of Nick Jensen's voice made her knees weak with relief, but she managed a feeble smile as she turned to him.

"Hi, Nick."

"Did I scare you?" he asked; his eyes searched her face in the moonlight. He offered his hand as she stood. After a slight hesitation, she placed her hand in his and he pulled her to her feet.

"Just a little. I didn't hear you come up."

"I'm sorry. I guess it is a little frightening out here alone at night." He grinned. "The city's full of ghosts, I hear."

Milton growled, eyes going from Jenny to Nick, who still held her hand in his. With an apologetic grimace, Nick let hers go and waved his so the dog could see they were empty.

With watchful eyes, Milton situated himself between them as if daring Nick to come too close to her.

"It's okay, Milt," Jenny soothed, patting the dog's head. Then, to Nick, "He's very protective."

"So, I see," Nick agreed, eyeing the dog warily.

"I don't think I've ever been so glad for spring break to get here," she said.

"Do you have any plans for your time off? Visiting family, taking a trip, or anything?"

"No." She had no family to visit. Her parents weren't the type that wanted her to visit often. They were busy with their own lives and had little in common with the daughter who shunned their lifestyle and money to make her own way. And taking a trip alone was too frightening an idea to even consider. "I guess I'm just going to relax at home."

"Good plan. Maybe we can get together," he suggested nonchalantly.

16

She was prepared to reject the idea, but when she met his eyes, the uncertainty she saw there moved her to nod her head in agreement. "Yeah, maybe so."

"Great," he agreed, "I'll call you."

Shocked at herself, she bid him a quiet good night before turning back toward her house.

Nick watched her walk away and wondered for the thousandth time why she tried so hard to hide how pretty she was. He had to admit it worked pretty well. Her bleached hair frizzing out in every direction always made him think of his four-year-old nieces' Barbie dolls. Trying to be beauticians like their mom, Molly and Macy had cut the dolls' hair into a ragged bob, before washing it with bath soap. By the time the impromptu make-overs were done, Barbie looked like she stuck her finger in a light socket and her head in wet cement. Would Jenny find that comparison insulting or would she be glad she had managed to do what he suspected she meant to do?

He had spent more of the last year than he cared to admit trying to imagine what she would look like under those shapeless, nondescript clothes and huge, slightly tinted, black-rimmed glasses she wore. Was she thin or shapely? Was she a natural blonde or brunette? He could almost imagine her as a redhead. Were her eyes brown or green behind those glasses? Or were they some fascinating combination of the two? Did her hips sway gently beneath the fabric of her skirt or did she move with a dignified glide?

He shook his head at his own foolishness and walked toward his own house. He needed a hobby. He was becoming obsessed with this silliness. If she didn't want anyone to know what she really looked like, if she wanted to be unattractive, that was her business. What drove him crazy was that even with the dowdy clothes and the untamed hair, she wasn't unattractive. Something about her still beckoned him.

Jenny was still stunned at her answer when she arrived home, her mind awhirl with thoughts of Nick and her semi-promise to get together over spring break. What in the world had come over her?

17

Without thought, she went to the cabinet and took down two bowls and filled them with colorful, presweetened cereal. As she took the gallon of milk from the refrigerator on the way to Milton sat by the table, his eyes moving from her face to the box in her hand as if questioning her choice for supper.

"Dinner's ready," she said as she set one bowl on his mat by the door and took the other to the table.

Every female on campus was smitten with Nick Jensen, herself included. No matter how she tried, she couldn't ignore him any more than she could ignore the sun when it finally appeared after days of rain.

Sometimes, she felt like a riddle Nick was trying to solve. He would look at her and she would feel as if he could see straight through her. Past the clothes and the horrible hairstyle, to the woman she was; a woman who sometimes wanted so badly to come out from behind the mask she wore; a woman who was once marked for death by a madman and was trying desperately to remain nondescript and anonymous so nothing like that ever happened again.

# CHAPTER FIVE

Jenny secured her frizzy blond hair with a barrette and grimaced before turning away from the bathroom mirror.

She fought the sudden and unfamiliar urge to take out the lipstick she had hidden at the very back of the drawer under the sink. What would it hurt to color her lips a nice petal pink? It had been nearly six years. Would anyone really recognize her if they saw her now? If she just used the lipstick, would it open their eyes to see past the wild hair and frumpy clothes to the twenty-two year old girl she had been when he took her? Would *he* see her and know who she was?

In the end, she slammed the drawer and stormed from the bathroom, angry with herself for being so foolish. She had worked years to perfect her protective covering; she would not ruin it now. What was wrong with her?

Even as the question entered her mind, his face was already forming before her. Nick Jensen. No matter how many times she told herself she wanted to remain plain old Jenny, she longed for him to see her as an attractive, desirable woman.

She smoothed a hand over the drab green sweater that hung well past her hips to the pleated black skirt that almost touched the top of her sensible black shoes, masking the shapely curves beneath. The unflattering style worked well with the thick-rimmed glasses to make her as nondescript as possible. The first thing she bought when she left the hospital six years ago was colored contacts that changed the unusual blue-green of her irises to a dull hazel. That alone may have been enough, but she was too desperate for anonymity to risk it. She would be a fool to let her guard down now.

With a pat on Milton's head, she locked the door behind her and headed for her car.

"Jenny!" Ellie Carson called from the yard next door. "Did your friend find you yesterday?"

"My friend?" Jenny repeated in puzzlement. Who would be looking here for her? Besides Ellie, all her acquaintances would have an easier time finding her at the school.

"Yes, tall, dark, handsome. He came by yesterday afternoon when I was weeding the flower bed. He knocked, but when you weren't home, he asked me if this was your house. He was a real dreamboat, I tell you."

"I have no idea who it might have been," Jenny said, but the pretty blonde just laughed.

"Whatever." Ellie shrugged, but her eyes were bright with curiosity. "You don't have to tell me if you don't want to. I'm just glad to see you coming out of your shell, even if it seems a bit unfair that you have that great-looking guy *and* Nick Jensen interested in you."

"Where in the world did you hear that?" Jenny asked in surprise, momentarily forgetting the man Ellie had spoken to the day before.

"About Nick?" Ellie laughed as Jenny stared at her. "The whole neighborhood knows it, Jenny. He hasn't made any real secret out of it."

"Why in the world would he be interested in me?" Jenny croaked.

"Men like a good mystery." Ellie said with a grin.

"Oh, for heaven's sake, Ellie. I'm about as mysterious as a rock." Jenny shook her head and laughed. "I have to get to the shop. I'll see you later."

Ellie was still smiling as she turned back to fertilizing her roses. It was about time Jenny saw some action, even if the poor woman wasn't certain she was ready for it. Ellie couldn't imagine a better way for her to get ready than to have two handsome men vying for her attention.

She had been trying for years to find Jenny a husband. It drove Jenny crazy, but she went along with it in her usual good-natured way, spending many a Sunday afternoon at Ellie's house talking to some bachelor Ellie had decided was perfect for her.

So far, none of them had ever talked Jenny into going on an actual date, but there had been one or two she saw again in Ellie's presence, whether at a football game, a social function, or something else with a large group of people. From what she could tell, Jenny was petrified at the thought of being alone with a man.

She wondered what made Jenny so wary of men, but she didn't want to jeopardize their friendship by asking questions about a subject Jenny obviously wanted to keep a secret. Ellie often wanted to ask Jenny what had happened to

She'd asked Ed what he thought, but he jokingly told her to quit reading so many novels, they were making her paranoid. She had agreed maybe she was seeing something that wasn't really there and left it up to Jenny to tell her anything she wanted to. Of course, no explanations were forthcoming.

A little thrill of hope danced through her as she remembered the blush that had crept across Jenny's cheeks at her mention of Nick Jensen. Obviously, the attraction was mutual, even if Jenny didn't want to admit it.

She smiled as she looked up at the sky. If the weather held, this weekend might be the perfect time for a neighborhood barbecue.

Jenny leaned into the trunk of her car, trying to reach the spool of ribbon that had fallen out of the box and rolled up behind the seats.

"Do you need some help, Miss Lewis?" Jenny pulled back, knocking her head on the roof of her car. "Oh!"

Looking over her shoulder, she saw a tall, blond student, leaning against the car behind her. She would swear he was looking at her butt, except that she knew exactly how unattractive it was in the pleated polyester skirt.

"No thanks, Kevin. I've got it," she said over her shoulder as her hand clasped the ribbon and she tossed it back in the box.

"All right then. See ya Monday." He shrugged and ambled down the street.

21

She was lifting the box out of the trunk when Nick pulled up behind her. Jumping out of his blue pickup, he hurried up to her.

"Let me get that, Jen."

"Thanks, but I can carry it." She tried to hold onto the box, but he easily took it out of her arms.

"Where does it need to go?"

"Nina's Needle. Nick, honestly, I can carry it," she protested as he strode toward the shop on the opposite side of the street.

"I have it and I'm carrying it. What kind of man wouldn't go out of his way for a pretty woman?"

The sound she made told him exactly what she thought of his compliment.

He stopped and turned toward her, glaring at her over the box.

"You are pretty," he said quietly. "I can't figure out why you work so hard not to be, but you'll tell me one day."

Her eyes widened behind her glasses and her bottom teeth worried her top lip for a moment as she stared at him.

"Just hurry up," she grumbled as she pushed past him to open the door of the shop.

"Set it on the counter."

He brushed against her on his way into the small, upscale shop, and her breath caught in her throat at the casual brushing of his arm against her. Heat prickled through her, tightening her stomach with desire, and she leaned against the door for a moment, praying for some semblance of order to her thoughts. What in the world was wrong with her? Before she could gather her wits, he was back, brushing past her on his way out.

"Bye, Jen," his voice held the barest suggestion of knowledge and her eyes shot open, meeting his dark, smiling ones.

"Bye, Nick." She frowned at the soft breathlessness of her own voice. She sounded like a lovesick teenager.

Disgusted with herself and her reaction to the man, she busied herself with emptying the box.

"What did you bring me today, Honey?" The tiny Bahamian woman who owned the shop peered over Jenny's shoulder.

"Fabric."

"Well, of course it's fabric, girl. But what kind?" Nina asked, hands on her hips.

Jenny pulled out the next bolt of cloth from the box and held it up.

"Ah, it's beautiful, Genevieve." Nina smiled in approval.

Nina had been her nanny from the time she was two years old, and Jenny loved her like a mother. When she started modeling and moved from Central Florida, Nina had moved with her, taking the place of Jenny's own mother. When Jenny relocated to St. Augustine, Nina followed. Jenny leased the shop where Nina sold the clothes she created, and Nina lived in the small upstairs apartment.

"This will be perfect," the dainty old woman said as she dreamily fingered the turquoise silk.

"For what?" Jenny asked, sensing that Nina's creativity was already at work designing the perfect use for the luxurious material.

"That's a secret, girl," Nina said with a sly smile as she carried the silk into the back room of the shop.

Jenny followed her, enjoying the breathtaking creations that hung around Nina's workroom. After laying the turquoise silk on her work table, Nina headed to the small dinette table at the back of the room. She took a seat and motioned for Jenny to do the same.

"Now," she said as she peered across the table at Jenny, "tell me about this gorgeous man who carried my material in for you this morning."

Jenny felt the telltale heat on her cheeks as she shook her head and poured herself a cup of tea from the kettle on the table.

"There's nothing to tell."

"Isn't there?" Nina asked, cocking her head to one side

"His name is Nick Jensen. He's the coach at the high school."

"And you like him?" Nina prodded.

Jenny shook her head vehemently, but stopped when she caught Nina's skeptical look.

"A little," she admitted and Nina nodded.

"And he likes you?"

"Yes."

"And you will date him?"

"No!" Jenny denied quickly.

"Yes," Nina said with an encouraging grin.

Jenny shrugged. "Maybe," she conceded.

"Good. You are young, Genevieve, too young to be alone. I want to see you happy before I die."

"I am happy. And don't talk about dying," Jenny admonished.

"You are not happy enough, child. And we will all die. That's why we must find happiness while we are alive."

Jenny shuddered as Nina spoke. Nina was right; she was lonesome lately. When she lay in bed at night with Milt at her feet, she dreamed of someone to hold her. She shook her head slightly, thinking of all the years she had wanted the same thing. Even as a child, she had longed for someone to love her, someone to hold her and make her feel like she mattered. Nina had done that for her when she was five years old and her parents had begun taking longer and longer trips to the Mediterranean. They had never been home much, never had vast amounts of time for their only child, but it got worse as she got older. By the time she graduated from high school, she only saw them about once a year. It had been three years since she had seen them last.

Even now, at twenty-eight, she was always surprised at how badly she missed them.

"Your mama wrote me, she says they'll be here in the States in the next few weeks," Nina said, patting Jenny's hand comfortingly.

Jenny wasn't surprised by Nina's words. The woman knew her better than anyone else and always recognized her longing for her parents.

"It's been a while since I saw them," she said quietly as she studied her hands, her parents' rejection as vivid now as it had ever been.

"Yes. But they'll be here soon."

"Why didn't she write me?" Jenny knew she sounded like an out-of-sorts child, but she couldn't help wondering why her mother would write Nina but not her own child.

Nina shrugged.

"You know your mama, child. She'll write you. Be patient."

Jenny nodded. She did know her mother. She knew her well enough to know that Helena Lewiston simply hadn't thought about writing to her daughter.

Suddenly filled with melancholy, Jenny stood up and moved toward the bolts of cloth that were stacked on the shelves across the room. She touched one, feeling the smooth coolness of the burnt orange satin. Gold highlights shot through it and Jenny could imagine the form-fitting sheath that Nina would create with it. She held it up to her face and walked toward the mirror that hung on the wall. It stood out too brilliantly against her pale skin and blond hair.

"That color always makes me think of you," Nina said as she rose from the tale. "There was a time that would have looked beautiful on you."

Jenny couldn't ignore the soft reproach in Nina's voice.

"I can't help it, Nina. You know I can't go back to being her again."

Nina cupped Jenny's face in her hands.

"Ah, Genevieve. I know you can never be her again, but you can be yourself again. You've not been yourself in a long, long time, child."

Nina studied the girl she loved as if she were her own. It broke her heart what that crazy person had done to her baby. He had almost killed her, but it was what he had taken from her that made Nina the angriest.

He had killed the calm self-assurance that had always been Genevieve's, the natural beauty that God had blessed her with, and the exuberant joy with which she had once faced each day.

She remembered the first time she ever saw the beautiful little girl with blue-green eyes that shone with inquisitiveness. She had been amazed at the child's ability to adjust to her parents' indifference. Although there were times when Nina saw the hurt in the child's eyes, Genevieve had seldom dwelt on it. She had been happy whether her parents were there with her or not, and had never let their apathy deter her.

Then had come the night Genevieve didn't return home. When they found her three days later, she was not the same girl who had left home that bright spring morning. She was broken and bruised and in the six years since, she had never completely healed.

Until today, Nina had not seen anyone look at her girl and see past the quiet, frumpy woman who stood before her to the woman who dwelt within. But she saw the way that handsome young man looked at her, saw the admiration in his eyes for what it was. This man, this Nick Jensen, saw the Genevieve she saw. He didn't see this woman before her or the beautiful make-believe Butterfly Girl she had been. Nick Jensen saw the Genevieve that had nearly been destroyed.

"I'll make you something out of this," Nina announced and held up the orange satin. "When you're ready, you'll have it to wear."

"Ready for what?"

"Ready to go out with that handsome boy who carried the box in," Nina said matter-of-factly.

Genevieve's laugh was uncharacteristically harsh. "Don't waste your material on me, Nina. I am not going out with him. And even if I did, he'd have to take me as I am or leave me be."

"I don't think he'll be leaving you, girlie. I think you'll have a hard time convincing that one that you won't go out with him."

Did she really want to convince Nick she wouldn't go out with him? Jenny wondered as she worked in the back room of the shop. Maybe Nina was right and it was time she thought about dating.

She didn't want to be alone forever, did she? Unable to answer her own questions, she folded the material and stuck it back on the shelf. She worked in silence straightening the bolts of cloth. As the bell to the front door rang, Nina hurried to the front of the shop to assist the customer who had entered.

The bell ran again and Nina's greeting was followed by a deep male voice.

"Jenny," the deep voice spoke from behind her and she swung around.

Nick stood at the doorway, the luxurious swathes of brightly hued material cascading from the walls behind him making him look even more masculine than normal. Attraction arced between them, leaving her breathless in its wake.

"What are you doing here?" she asked, trying to sound as if the answer didn't really matter to her.

"I thought I'd see if you wanted to get some lunch." His eyes moved to her mouth, and she licked her lips nervously.

"No," she said impatiently. "I'm busy."

"Can't you leave for a little while?" he insisted.

"No, Nick, I can't. Nina needs me to do this."

"Do you work here?" he asked, looking around as if he were trying to determine what she did there.

"No, I don't work here." She started to explain to him about Nina and the shop, but fought the urge and clamped her mouth shut. The less she explained the better.

He moved closer to her, reaching over her shoulder to pull a bolt of cloth from the shelf.

"I'll bet this would look gorgeous on you," he said quietly.

She looked down at the material, expecting a pale blue or pink. She sucked in her breath as she stared down at the burnt orange and gold satin she had just replaced. Her eyes flew to his face and she felt the tendrils of fear flame to life inside of her. Unconsciously, she began to back away, her heart pounding in her chest.

He knew! Somehow he knew.

"Jenny, what's wrong?" Worry tinged his words.

"You know," she whispered.

"No, I don't know."

"Why would you say that would look good on me?"

He placed the material on the table, and took a step toward her.

"I don't know. You were standing there and it was behind you and I thought it was pretty. I thought it would look pretty on you. Add some color to your wardrobe."

His confusion seemed so genuine she heaved a huge sigh of relief and sank into the nearest chair. She had to get a grip on her paranoia, and maybe the best way to do that was to face it head on.

"Where did you want to go for lunch?" she asked, hoping she didn't sound as frightened as she felt.

27

Jenny was driving home from the shop before she remembered the man Ellie had said stopped by her house. Ellie's description had left quite a lot to be desired. Tall, dark and handsome? She racked her brain for any other man she knew who Ellie could compare to Nick. Suddenly, it came to her. There had only been one other man in her life that was tall, dark and handsome. Only one man who would have searched her out in her new life and there would only be one reason he would do so.

Either they had finally caught her assailant or he had struck again. Either way, Sam must have come to warn her that her nightmare was about to start all over.

# CHAPTER SIX

May 1, 2003
Steinhatchee, Florida
Anna Blue, *Lycaeides idas anna*

*Anna Steinberg walked into Martine's in a stunning blue dress, and he couldn't help but think that it was surely a sign.*

*He first saw the blond, blue-eyed news anchor on the evening news and couldn't help but notice her ethereal beauty. When her name appeared at the bottom of the screen, he began making his plans.*

*He followed her for a few days to learn her habits. Every night at seven thirty, she ate at Martine's bar and grill. On the fourth night, he ate there, too. He positioned himself at the bar so that she could see him from her spot on the opposite end. He knew the moment she saw him. Her eyes lit up like sapphires and she gave him a winning smile as he met her gaze.*

*They had dined together every night since, and in that week, he learned a lot about her. He knew she had been married to a sorry excuse for a human who abused her regularly, but was now divorced. Her children were living with her mother in Omaha while she got settled in Florida, and would join her once the school year was over.*

*All alone for the moment, the loneliness shone like a beacon in her eyes, and he did his best to make her think he was the answer to her pain..*

*As she slipped into her seat at the table, he smiled. "I hope you don't mind, but I ordered for you. If we eat quickly, we might not miss watching the sunset on the beach."*

*"That would be lovely."*

*The beach was empty and the sun was setting slowly in a haze of gold and pink when Anna fell prey to the drug. Her half-empty wine glass slipped from her hand, its deep burgundy contents spilling to the sand. Her body tilted toward him, and he caught her, laying her back as he went to his car for the things he would need.*

*He spread the clear plastic out on the beach, then gently picked her up and placed her on it. Her eyes were wide and frightened as he crossed her arms over her chest and placed the small white butterfly there. He wrapped the plastic around her body, imprisoning her in a thick plastic cocoon.*

*"Sleep well, Anna Blue," he whispered as he sealed the plastic over her face. "You will awake transformed."*

*Later that night, as he stood before Vanessa's butterfly collection, he stared into the case that held the lone black and red butterfly. With trembling hands, he pinned a tiny butterfly, identical to the one he had left with Anna Steinberg, onto the velvet beside Vanessa's.*

# CHAPTER SEVEN

Ellie's teenage son, Derek, waved from next door as Jenny pulled into her drive. She smiled wistfully as he got into a car full of teenagers that waited on the narrow street, although she had no idea if she longed to be that young and carefree again or if it was the full life Ellie had with her two sons and adoring husband.

She usually didn't mind the quiet emptiness of her house, but today it seemed a little too quiet and empty to bear. The clock on her dashboard said she was home earlier than usual. Maybe Ellie wouldn't mind her coming over to talk after she took Milton for a walk.

Milton was waiting in front of the door, his leash in his mouth, when she walked through the door.

"I guess this means you're ready for a walk," she said as she clipped the leash to his collar.

Today they took a more circuitous route, going several blocks west of the house and cutting across the playground full of children. She slowed to watch them play on the jungle gym and slide. Their noisy play made her suddenly long for the noise of children to fill her home.

Shocked by her train of thoughts, she picked up her pace, leaving the playground behind as she considered the possibility that she'd had some sort of mental break. How else could she explain her sprint from admitting a man was handsome and interesting to longing for children?

"You, too, huh?" she said to the dog who pulled at his leash and whined insistently, longing to join the fray on the playground. "C'mon, Milt, let's go home."

He followed her, casting an occasional backward glance at the playground. Usually, she would let him play. He loved it when she let the kids throw his worn yellow tennis ball around for him to retrieve, but amidst the barrage of unfamiliar feelings that assailed her, she suddenly longed for the familiarity and safety of her own home.

She couldn't help but cast a glance toward Nick's house as they passed. After all, it must be why she decided to come the long way around, even if she didn't want to admit it. Neither he nor his truck were anywhere in sight, and she breathed a sigh of relief. What kind of idiocy led a grown woman to casually saunter past a man's house for no reason except to get a glimpse of him?

Disappointment surged through her when she turned the corner and saw that Ellie's gray minivan was no longer parked in the driveway. She really needed to discuss her unfamiliar obsession with someone.

She glanced at the bed and breakfast across the street from her house. Baskets of fern and bright pink begonias hung heavy from the porch of the large, cream-colored Victorian and near the front door, a large wooden plaque read, "La Cosecha Inn". There were several cars pulled into the small paved drive and another parked on the road in front of the bougainvillea-covered fence. The first week of spring break, and the place was already packed.

A bright green slip of paper waved happily from her front door and she shook her head in exasperation as she read the note. Ellie was having a barbeque Sunday at two in the afternoon. Nick would be there and Ellie expected Jenny to be there, all dolled up, a half hour early.

Ellie was up to her usual matchmaking. Jenny should be used to it, but something about Nick being the other target made her nervous. She suspected anything that developed between them would change both their lives forever.

She grabbed a bottle of water from the refrigerator and was searching the freezer for anything that sounded good for supper, when someone knocked at the front door. Milt began barking furiously, rushing between her and the door.

"Shush, Milton," she ordered.

Expecting Ellie to have come by to confirm she saw the note, she threw open the door.

"Really, El –"

32

In the back of her mind, she had always known he would be there one day. She had prayed she was wrong, hoped never to see him again, but here he was, a living, breathing reminder of all she wished she could forget.

"Sam," she said quietly, her voice seeming to desert her.

"You look great, Genevieve" he said with a teasing grin, his dark eyes raking her over from head to toe. He was at least a decade older than her, but still one of the best-looking men she'd ever seen. "May I come in?"

She warred with the idea of simply slamming the door in his face and pretending he had never come. In the end, however, she knew she had to hear what he had come to say, so with a defeated smile she motioned him in.

In the living room, she sat on one end of the sofa and pulled her feet up under her, while he sat in an easy chair across from her.

"So, you're still teaching, I see," he observed as his eyes fell on the stack of tests waiting to be graded on her coffee table.

"Yes."

He looked around him and she realized suddenly that the always cool and calm Sam was nervous. The realization terrified her.

"There were a lot of folks out tonight. Guess the nice weather brought them out. I even saw a wedding in the gazebo."

"Sam, why are you here? You know I'm not naive enough to think you're here to talk about weather and weddings." She held up her hand as he started to speak. "Nor am I naïve enough to believe you're here just to see me."

"Good Lord, Jenny, when did you get so cynical?" he asked, eyes sparking with humor.

"About the same time some loon wrapped me up in plastic and dumped me by the river." She sat forward hopefully. "Did they catch him?"

He shook his head and she pursed her lips, fighting the tears she felt burning the back of her eyes. She knew he wouldn't have come unless it was something bad. From the indecipherable look in his eyes, it just might be something horrible.

"Jenny." His voice was soft, but the words hit her like blows. "We discovered a link between your case and a series of murders around the state. They started in two-thousand and three. I don't know why it took so long to make the connection."

"How many?" she choked out, feeling as if the breath was knocked out of her.

"Ten."

"Oh, my God," she whispered as the world shifted and careened around them.

He met her horrified gaze and swallowed hard.

"How do you know it's the same person?"

"His signature is always the same. Ten women, all killed the beginning of May, wrapped in plastic and left in out of the way places from here to the Keys. Every one of them has been just like your case, Genevieve, right down to the butterfly on her chest."

The orange and brown butterfly that had been pinned to her chest had led the police to assume the attempt on her life was linked to her association with Butterfly Cosmetics. But an obsessed fan wouldn't have killed nine other women.

"Why a butterfly?" she asked.

"We don't know. Apparently, the butterflies are a very integral part of the murders, but no one has found the connection yet. They've called in the Feds and their profiler believes the plastic represents a chrysalis or cocoon. The only thing we know for sure is that the crimes are connected and almost definitely committed by the same person."

"How long has this been happening?"

"The first victim was found in Steinhatchee in two thousand three."

"Two thousand and three?" she cried in disbelief. "Ten years?"

"Like I said, they've happened all over Florida. They started in Steinhatchee and the last body was found near Panama City. There has been one in Miami, one in Tampa, and everywhere in between. We may never have linked them if it wasn't for this last one. It was a little different than the others."

She looked at him questioningly and he went on.

34

"He left a note with this one. It told us about the other murders. It also told us he needs you to complete the circle. If we don't produce you when he tells us to, he swears he'll kill a girl every week until we do."

"Why would he want me again?"

"I don't know, maybe because you escaped or maybe because you were the Butterfly Girl. I can't say, but judging from the things he says, he knows where you are, Jenny. He knows who you are, but he doesn't want *this* version of you. He wants the former version. He wants the Butterfly Girl."

"Oh, God," Jenny repeated in horror, hiding her face in her hands. She prayed that this wasn't real, that Sam would disappear and that all of this would just be a bad dream. When she opened her eyes, he still sat there, a benevolent looking bearer of devastating news.

"You don't have to do it, Jen," he offered. "I wouldn't blame you if you refused."

"How can you even think I would refuse?" she cried, offended that he would think she would sentence another girl to the hell she'd endured. "A girl a week? For how long? Until you catch him or until he has me? You've had six years to catch him since me, Sam. That's an awful lot of weeks. An awful lot of girls. I'm not willing to risk that."

"I knew you wouldn't be." He stood up, waving her to sit back down when she tried to stand. "We'll do everything we can to protect you and keep you safe."

"I need time to think, Sam."

"Take a few days, make sure you're up to this. I'll call you in a few days, but in the meantime, be vigilant and keep your eyes open." He bent and placed a soft kiss on the top of her head. "Lock the door behind me."

# CHAPTER EIGHT

May 1, 2004
Tampa, Florida
Stella Orangetip, *Anthocharis stella*

    *Stella Dobbins stepped from the bus and hurried toward the elderly couple waiting at the station for her. She kissed her father's papery cheek then turned to embrace her mother, a much older version of Stella herself.*

    *On the two-hour bus ride to Tampa, he'd learned she was visiting her parents, who had moved to Florida from Pennsylvania when they retired three years ago. Everything else she'd said fled his mind as he watched her, mesmerized by the gracefulness of each movement she made, from the way she craned her long slender neck toward her parents, to how her hands moved like slender wings as she spoke. As the last passenger stepped onto the bus, he slipped out the door. He said nothing to her as he motioned for one of the taxis waiting there and had the driver wait until Stella and her parents pulled away. The taxi followed them as far as their driveway before heading to the nearest hotel.*

    *He watched her for three days before he knocked on her parents' door.*

    *"Hi," she said, a soft smile spreading across her pretty face when she pulled the door open. "What are you doing here?"*

    *"I kept thinking of you, of how much I enjoyed talking to you on our ride down. I want to get to know you better." He smiled the smile Vanessa had always told him would melt women's hearts. "Would you like to go on a date or two? See what happens from there?"*

    *He realized long ago how amazingly easy it was to flatter a woman into forgetting he was a stranger. It was especially easy if the woman was in a vulnerable time her life.*

There were some women who were always vulnerable, but nervous weepy types took the fun right out of the game. Those types were too fragile to be a butterfly.

Others were never vulnerable, always rough and tough, and impossible to make a butterfly.

The ideal women were the ones who weren't always vulnerable, but were made that way by the circumstances of the moment. Divorcees feeling unattractive and desperate for love; women who had experienced a huge loss in their loss in their lives, a parent, spouse, child; or women like Stella, who found they were suddenly facing middle age without ever having known the love of a husband or child.

He had seen the vulnerability in Stella's golden eyes the moment they met his on the bus. She knew her time was running out. She was nearing fifty years old, too old to be a mother, too young to completely give up hoping she might still meet the perfect man. All he had to do was become that perfect man. For two weeks, he courted her. He was her soul mate, the man she had dreamed of for forty-eight years.

He made sure that their last night together was all she could ever have wanted. It was perfect, with the cool spring air blowing around them as they ate on the deck of a casually elegant restaurant overlooking the ocean. He could see the happiness in her eyes. She thought all her dreams were coming true.

He made certain the hotel room he rented would continue the aura of romance he created. The last thing he wanted was a fight on his hands. He needed her to believe the illusion until the very last moment.

He ordered champagne and poured them both a glass before joining her on the big king bed. They sat with their backs against the headboard as he proposed a toast.

"To you, Stella" he said touching his glass to hers. "Just the woman I've been looking for."

She smiled brightly and answered in kind. "I've searched for you for years."

She took a sip of champagne, then another. By the third, her hands grew weak and he plucked the glass from her hand before *she dropped it. Her body became limp and pliant while her eyes burned with fear.*

*He carried her downstairs, nuzzling her neck when they passed a group of partygoers in the hallway. Let them think the two of them with lovers overcome with passion. A few disapproving glances were better than anyone realizing the truth.*

*In the empty parking lot, he laid her on the plastic that was spread there, placed the gray butterfly with orange wingtips on her chest and wrapped her snugly. He drove to the spot he'd chosen in the Everglades, right off the Tamiami Trail, and lifted her from the trunk.*

*He could feel that she had shifted in her cocoon, perhaps even tried to break free, but in the end, she had succumbed just as Anna Steinberg had, and one more butterfly was added to Vanessa's collection.*

# CHAPTER NINE

"Jenny, it's Ellie, pick up the phone. I know you're home. I can see your car in the drive. Okay, fine, ignore me for now, but you can't ignore me forever. I'm going to keep calling until you get so annoyed you have to answer."

Jenny lay in her bed listening to the answering machine.

Ellie had been calling since eight o'clock this morning. At noon, she'd come over and beat on the door. Since then, she'd called a dozen times. At first, she wanted to know if Jenny was angry that she invited Nick to the barbecue. Now, she just wanted to know Jenny was okay.

The phone rang again and Jenny thought longingly about smashing it to bits with a hammer.

"Jenny, this is Nick Jensen. Ellie just called me. She's worried to death about you. She says you aren't speaking to her. I don't know why she thinks you would answer the phone for me and not her, but if she hasn't heard back from you or me in ten minutes, she's calling the paramedics. Are you hurt, are you not able to come to the phone, or are you just being hardheaded? If you want to save your front door from the battering ram, I'd suggest you call your friend."

Jenny chuckled quietly as the message ended and she punched in Ellie's number.

"Jenny?" Ellie yelled into the phone.

"I'm fine. I'm not mad. I'm not hurt. And I'm not dead. So don't call the paramedics."

"What's going on then?" Ellie demanded in an injured tone.

"It's a long story, El."

"I'll be right over."

The phone clicked in Jenny's ear before she could tell Ellie not to come. Ellie was already knocking on the door before Jenny had hung up the phone. Sam would be furious if she told Ellie the truth, but she wasn't sure she could contain it any longer. Ellie was the closest friend she had, and although she debated ignoring her persistent knocking, in the end, Jenny opened the door and let her in.

"You were the Butterfly Girl?" Ellie screeched a few minutes later. "Jeez Louise, what did you do to yourself?"

"I guess that means the disguise worked." Jenny ran her hand self-consciously over her frizzy hair.

"Sorry, Jen, I always figured a makeover would do wonders for you, but I had no idea it would turn you into the girl that stole the heart of every teenage boy in America ten years ago."

"I know it's hard to believe, but it's true."

"I don't understand why you're telling me this know, though. What does it have to do with you locking yourself in your house for two days?"

"I've been asked to be the Butterfly Girl again."

"Jenny! That's great! Are they going to give you a makeover?"

Jenny nodded silently, fear clogging her throat at the thought.

"What's wrong?" Ellie's eyes narrowed as she waited for Jenny to answer. "Does this have something to do with that good-looking guy who was looking for you?

Jenny nodded again. Then, taking a deep breath she began to tell the rest of the story.

"Sam. His name is Sam Conway. He's a detective with the Brevard County Police Department."

"A detective?"

"Ellie, when I was doing the ads for Butterfly, I was kidnapped and left for dead. A fisherman found me two days later, wrapped in plastic with a dead butterfly on my chest. The police assumed the crime was connected to my job with Butterfly Cosmetics. There was never a suspect, no clues or anything else. After the investigation hit a dead end, I wanted nothing more than to disappear." She took a deep breath. "Sam helped make that happen."

She could still remember the debilitating fear that gripped her when she thought of walking out of the hospital after the attack. No matter how hard she tried, she couldn't force herself to move.

Luckily Sam took pity on her and came to the hospital with hair dye, a new wardrobe, and a ticket to her new identity. By the next morning, she was someone new, a woman who could easily blend in and never be noticed at all.

"So, is the case still open?" Ellie asked, interrupting her thoughts.

"It's been relegated to the cold case files all these years, but there have been some recent developments that made it into a much bigger case than anyone thought it was."

"Why?" Ellie eyes widened with fear.

"There was a recent murder, a girl found wrapped in plastic with a butterfly on her chest. With her, there was a note telling police about ten other murders all over the state. It also promised that if I, the only girl who ever got away from him, didn't reappear, he would start killing a girl a day until I did. He doesn't want me as I am now, though. He wants me as I was then. He wants the Butterfly Girl."

Silence reigned as the full weight of Jenny's words sunk in.

"What are you going to do?" Ellie finally whispered in despair. Her eyes welled with worried tears.

Jenny gave her friend a small, sad smile. "I'm going to get a makeover."

Both of them jumped at the sound of a fist pounding on the front door.

"Jenny!"

"Oh, no!" Ellie cried at the sound of the familiar masculine voice. She leapt from her seat. "I forgot to call Nick and tell him I talked to you! I called him practically hysterical
with worry."

"Make him go away!" Jenny hissed as she rushed into her bedroom and shut the door.

Ellie hurried to the front door, while Nick continued to pound on it.

43

Nick had waited for what seemed like an eternity for Ellie to call back. When she didn't, worry got the best of him and he'd run the three blocks between their house.

"I forgot to call you," Ellie said sheepishly as she opened the door.

"What's going on? Is she okay?" he demanded, pushing past her and striding into the living room. "Jenny!"

"Nick, you can't just barge in here."

"Hush, Ellie. Where is she?" His eyes honed in on her. "Why are you crying?"

"I'm not crying," she denied.

"I was married for three years, Ellie. You don't think I know when a woman is crying?"

"For goodness' sake, Nick. What is wrong?" Jenny asked from behind him.

He spun around, relief rushing through him when he saw her alive and well although obviously just as upset as Ellie appeared to be.

"What's wrong?" he repeated, his eyebrows lifting dramatically. "I get a call from a nearly hysterical woman this morning saying she hasn't seen you in days. She says you won't pick up the phone and you haven't left home. She was calling the police if you didn't answer again. So, I call. I get no answer. I call her house, and her son says she flew over here like a bat out of hell." Nick took a deep breath. "I was worried. That's what's wrong."

"Sorry, Nick," Ellie apologized, her face beaming despite his scowl.

"What's so darn funny?"

"Nothing," she grinned.

"Ellie," Jenny's voice held a warning that made him roll his eyes.

Great, now he recognized that grin. Ellie thought she had accomplished some great feat of matchmaking by making him run over here like a crazy person.

"Now that I know everyone's safe, I have to get home," Ellie announced, hugging Jenny before heading out the door. "Don't forget about my barbecue."

Nick studied Jenny for a few long moments. She was pale and worried looking, and he had to control the urge to reach for her hand.

"What's going on?" he asked gently.

"Honestly, it's no big deal. I've just been feeling a little down the past couple of days."

"Are you sure that's it?"

"Yes. Ellie overreacted, as usual."

He was far from convinced, but he would give her the benefit of the doubt.

"Well, I really have a lot to do. I'll see you at Ellie's tomorrow afternoon."

He shook his head in discouragement as he followed her to the door. Were they ever going to get past this stage? Was he ever going to get more than a polite rejection? Sometimes, he thought he saw real interest in her eyes, times when he thought she may be attracted to him. But there were far more times like this, when she smiled with feigned interest and then kindly pushed him away.

"You'll be at Ellie's?" he verified before she shut the door in his face.

"Of course. She'd never forgive me if I weren't."

"She's trying to fix us up, you know."

"I know," she smiled indulgently toward Ellie's house. "She's hopelessly optimistic."

"Are you?"

"Not anymore." She smiled sadly as she closed the door between them.

# CHAPTER TEN

Nick watched Ellie scurry around, laughing and talking with her guests, making sure the trays of food and coolers full of drinks never emptied. She seemed as normal as ever, but he would swear every time her gaze drifted to where Jenny sat in the shade of the huge oak tree, her eyes filled with tears. She would quickly disappear into the house or around the side of the yard, only to reappear in a few moments with her normal bright, if somewhat strained, smile on her face.

She had just repeated the scenario for at least the tenth time and was stepping into the kitchen when Nick decided enough was enough. He followed her through the door and was witness to the way she leaned against the wall, taking a deep fortifying breath before dashing the tears from her eyes and pasting the smile on her face once more. She jumped when she turned and found him between her and the door.

"What's going on, Ellie?" he demanded quietly.

Her smile grew even bigger, brighter and more artificial.

"What do you mean?"

"Is something wrong with Jenny?"

"No, of course not." Her smile was going to crack her face. She looked around his shoulder, desperation in her eyes as she searched for a way out.

"You're a terrible liar, Ellie."

The smile slipped from her face and she leaned back against the wall.

"I know. I always have been."

His stomach dropped at the tears that pooled in her eyes.

"Is she sick? Dying? Good Lord, Ellie, you can't even look at her without crying, so I know it's bad."

"Jenny has to be the one to tell you, Nick. I can't."

"She won't. I've already asked."

"Give her time. She's still working it out in her mind. She'll tell you when the time is right. Just be patient with her." A genuine smile crossed her face. "You really do like her, don't you?"

"Oh, yeah," he admitted, gazing at a distant point behind Ellie's shoulder. "I've been crazy about her since the moment I met her."

"I knew it!"

"There's something irresistible about her. Beauty so deep, so basic that I can't ignore it. I don't even think she realizes it."

"You should tell her that, Nick. Tell her today, before it's too –."

She bit off the last word, a look of horror crossing her pretty face as she clamped a hand over her mouth.

"Too late?" he finished, nearly choking on his words. "My God, she is dying."

"I hope not, Nick. God, I hope not."


Jenny sat under the tree, pretending to be enjoying herself, even though Sam's visit had left her cold and numb to nearly anything but the fear that consumed her.

Nick strode across the yard toward her, reminding her that she wasn't numb to him. She was more than a little attracted to him. Handsome, kind, and fun, Nick Jensen was everything she could ever want. She couldn't remember a time she had been more attracted to a man.

Even Sam never made her feel the way Nick did. Of course, she and Sam had never been real. Sam had never done more than make her want the temporary comfort he had offered; Nick, on the other hand, made her want it all. For a moment, she let herself imagine Nick pushing a baby stroller while the leaves changed and formed a colorful carpet across the neighborhood playground. She imagined him pushing a tire swing high in the air, while a dark-haired toddler laughed out loud and the azaleas bloomed along her back fence. She imagined snuggling up next to him on the sofa on a cold winter day.

48

Then, out of nowhere, she imagined the plastic winding its way around her face, sealing her in and the air out. And she knew in her heart that this was how it would be. There would be no husband, no children. There would be no forever. There were only the days until the killer decided it was time, and then she'd be dead.

Nick slid into the chair beside her, his eyes searching her face. She held her breath, waiting for him to demand answers to the questions in his gaze, but in the end, he just sat back, laying a hand across the back of her chair.

"Jenny, listen, we've been skirting around this for months. I've never hid my feelings for you and I hope you feel the same. I think it's time we took the next step. I want you to go out with me."

"I can't, Nick." She hadn't meant for her voice to sound so sad.

"Why?"

"I just can't," she repeated.

"Are you not attracted to me?"

Her laughter was soft and bitter. "You are a true idiot, Nick. Can't you see how attracted I am to you? I'm more than attracted to you actually. That's why I can't go out with you."

"That's the most ridiculous thing I've ever heard."

"There are things you just don't know."

"Tell me then," he pleaded, and for a moment, she was sorely tempted to obey.

"I can't."

He took her hand in his. "I want you to know that I think you're the most beautiful woman I've ever known."

She laughed and he glared at her.

"Maybe there are people who look at you and see only what you want them to see, but I see you, Jenny. I see beneath this disguise you wear, and I know down deep, where it counts, you are truly a beautiful woman."

With an anguished cry, she bounded from her seat and hurried through the yard, ignoring the looks the others cast her way

Safely locked inside her house, Jenny threw herself onto her bed and sobbed broken-heartedly. Why, after all these years of being alone, had she finally found the perfect man? He cared for her. He thought she was beautiful. Even without Butterfly

49

Cosmetics, he thought she was beautiful. Inside. Where it counted the most.

A few days ago, she'd been thinking seriously of going out with him. Now, there was no sense in it. There was no future. It would only bring him pain. She couldn't knowingly deceive him by acting like there was hope for them.

Milton whimpered and climbed on the bed beside her. She'd been crying off and on since Sam's visit. When she wasn't crying, she was moping around. No wonder Milton was so worried. They hadn't been for a walk since the night Sam had come to see her, so Milton was relegated to exercising in the back yard, while she hid away in the house.

As if reading her mind, Milt crawled over to the nightstand where she kept his leash and picked it up with his mouth. Turning his head, he dropped it beside her face. She looked at him guiltily, knowing how much he enjoyed their walks, but unwilling to oblige him today. There was a real chance she'd run into Nick today, and if not Nick, someone who had been at Ellie's party and witnessed her panicked escape.

"Not today, Sweetie. I can't face anyone today."

Like a child, Milt glared reproachfully at her for a moment, jumped from the bed and left the room without looking back.

She lay back with one arm over her face and closed her eyes. How could she ever face Nick again?

She was jerked awake by the ringing of the phone. She lay there silently, one arm covering her eyes, as the answering machine picked up.

"Jenny, please pick up," Nick pleaded. "I'm sorry if I rushed you."

He hung up and the phone rang again within seconds.

"Jenny, it's Ellie. What happened? He likes you. You like him. So, what's the problem?"

Jenny felt like screaming. Was Ellie completely in the dark? How could she not know what the problem was? Angrily, she snatched up the phone and pressed the button to turn off the machine before Ellie hung up.

"The problem is that I'm going to die soon. I'm going to become the freaking Butterfly Girl again, and then I'm going to be the sacrificial lamb so that some psycho won't go on killing women. I'll be dead, El, and where will that leave Nick Jensen?"

"Jenny, you don't know that. Surely the police are going to protect you. They can't truss you up like a Thanksgiving turkey and leave you on his doorstep."

"They won't have to, Ellie. He knows where I live. He knows who I am. He's just waiting to see if I'll come to him."

"What if you don't come to him?"

"He'll come to me. Either way, I'll be dead."

Ellie was silent for a moment. Then, with blunt honesty, she spoke quietly into the phone.

"You can't be dead if you were never alive, Jen."

# CHAPTER ELEVEN

Jenny spent the next day pacing the confines of her house and mulling over Ellie's words. She had been so stunned by the uncharacteristic cruelty she had replaced the receiver without any acknowledgement Ellie had spoken.

It was so close to what Nina had said a few days ago.

*We must find happiness while we are alive.*

*You can't be dead if you were never alive.*

The words played over and over in her head, Nina's softly accented voice, mingling with Ellie's slow, southern drawl. These were the two women who knew the most about her. Nina had known the child, the teenager, and, now, the woman. Ellie knew all there was to know about the woman she had become six years ago. Now, she even knew who she was before.

What did they both see in her to make them think she wasn't living her life to its advantage? Were they right?

As the rain that began that morning continued, she attempted to look over the essays her advanced twelfth grade English class had turned in. After reading the same sentence a dozen times, she stood up and went to the window.

The lights next door shone dimly through the shades, and she imagined Ellie and Ed sitting side by side, watching television in the living room. The boys were probably upstairs in their own rooms doing whatever teenage boys do in the privacy of their rooms. In the past six years, she had watched them live their lives to the fullest. She had watched pain hit them as Ed lost his mother to Alzheimer's and Ellie lost her father to cancer, and they had both taken on the new burden of caring for widowed parents who didn't know exactly what to do now that their spouses were gone.

She had watched the little boys who lived there become handsome young men. She knew Ellie caught the youngest, Eddie, smoking pot in his tree house two years ago, and that he continued to give them hell occasionally. She was a witness to the pain and anger that came with being parents of a rebellious child. She watched them love him and Derek anyway.

They didn't live exciting lives. They just lived a normal suburban life. But they lived. They didn't let anything get in their way of living or of loving each other. What would it be like to love and be loved so completely? Was it possible she and Nick could love each other that way? If she told him the truth would he be willing to love her for whatever time they had?

Her phone rang behind her and, once again, she let the answering machine pick it up.

"Tell him, Jen," Ellie said quietly.

Jenny looked up. She couldn't help but smile at Ellie who stood at her own kitchen window. Jenny inclined her head slightly and Ellie grinned. Ed appeared behind his wife, nuzzling her neck. She said something and he looked toward Jenny's house. With a smile and a wave, he led Ellie away from the window.

Jenny stood there for an instant before going into her bedroom. She took a small box from the top shelf of the closet and took out two folded newspapers. She scanned them, making sure they said only what she wanted to reveal. She would tell Nick the rest of her story when she got good and ready. With a sigh, she folded the papers, carried them into the living room and placed them on the bookshelf beside the television.

Taking a deep breath, she dialed Nick's number and asked him to dinner the following night. When he had overcome the shocked silence that followed her invitation, he agreed to be there at six.

54

# CHAPTER TWELVE

He arrived right on time, and as she hurried to answer the door, Jenny wondered wildly if she had done something totally insane by asking him over. She hadn't changed anything about the way she looked or dressed, although she had once again considered applying just a bit of makeup to her pale face. For a little longer, she would hide behind the comforting safety of her too-big dresses and too-thick glasses.

When she opened the door, he stood on the steps, a sheepish grin on his face and a bouquet of white daisies in his outstretched hand.

"These are from Ellie," he said under his breath, "but don't tell her I told you."

"I wouldn't dream of it." Jenny said with mock seriousness.

Looking over his shoulder, she saw Ellie standing beside her minivan with a bag of groceries in each arm. Ellie never came home from the grocery without a fresh bouquet of flowers, but today, there were none sticking out from either bag. She shook her head in exasperation as her ever-hopeful friend juggled her groceries in an attempt to give her an enthusiastic thumbs-up.

"You are hopeless!" she called, taking Nick's arm and pulling him inside.

"I think you mean hopeful!" Ellie answered with a laugh before Jenny shut the door.

"She's a real control freak," Jenny laughed, jerking her thumb toward Ellie's house. "Especially when she's playing matchmaker."

"Is that what she's doing?" he asked with feigned innocence as he followed her through the living room and into the kitchen.

"Yeah, and she thinks it's finally working." She bent to take the pan of lasagna out of the oven.

"Is it?"

"Maybe," she said with a shrug. She stood up and carried the pan to the table. "Grab that bowl of salad and I'll grab the bread."

As they ate, they made small talk. They talked about one of their students he felt was bound to win a scholarship to college and she agreed that he would do well there. Not only was he an extremely talented athlete, he was also highly intelligent and had a real talent for writing.

They moved on to family then. She smiled as he told her about his sister and brother, who he obviously loved dearly. He described growing up as part of the perfect middle class dream. She told him how it was to grow up the only child of rich, self-indulgent parents who moved to another country as soon as they thought she was old enough to live on her own. Finally, she told him about Nina and how the small Jamaican woman became so much like a mother to her.

He talked about playing sports as a child and in college and his decision to coach. She told him that books had been her only company the many days and nights that her parents were away. It had been a natural choice to go into teaching English and Literature.

When all the relatively safe subjects were exhausted, he told her about his short-lived marriage.

"It just didn't work out. I don't think either of us was ready for marriage. At least, not to each other. Corrine married someone else about six months after our divorce was final. She's been married to him for five years and has two kids. I see her every once in a while and she seems really happy. I guess I just wasn't the right man for her."

She detected the slight note of wistfulness in his voice and touched his hand gently.

"Do you still care for her?"

He quickly shook his head.

"No, well, yes, I mean, I'm happy for her. Envious, too, maybe. I guess we'd all like to find what she found."

Jenny nodded in understanding, thinking how many times in the past few days she had wished for the same things.

"It's funny, isn't it? How can we go through our days thinking we are doing exactly what we want and then, suddenly, something happens and we realize all we are doing is making do?"

"Is that what you're doing, Jenny? Making do until you find what you really want out of life?"

She shrugged. "I don't know. I like teaching, but I don't know that I like it so much I want it to be all I ever do."

"Do you want a family?" he asked. "Kids?"

She was silent for a minute, thinking of how much she had come to realize she wanted kids and a husband. Would her enthusiasm scare him away?

"I'd love to have a family," she admitted even as she resigned herself to the fact that she would probably never have either. "But I'm not sure it will ever happen."

"Why?" he asked with a puzzled frown. "You're still young enough. Anything could happen."

She remained silent, knowing this was the time to explain, but unable to utter the words.

"What's wrong, Jen?" he asked, running his eyes over her face.

Realizing her brow was creased into a worried frown, she forced herself to relax and smile at him.

"Nothing's wrong," she said and stood up from the table.

She quickly began stacking the dishes.

"Jenny, don't," he said quietly, putting a hand on her arm to stop her as she reached for his plate.

"I have to clear the table," she said, refusing to look at him.

"You know that's not what I mean." He bent toward the table and looked up at her. "Don't do this 'go away, Nick' thing you do."

"I didn't say I wanted you to go away," she denied as she turned away from him and carried the dishes to the sink.

"I know you didn't say it. You rarely say it. You don't have to."

"What are you talking about?" she asked with feigned ignorance as she watched the sink fill with hot soapy water.

He stood behind her and, feeling his presence, she lifted her head and her eyes met his reflection in the window above the sink.

His gaze was steady as he closed his hands around her upper arms and moved closer to her.

"You know what I'm talking about," he said quietly.

She began to shake her head in denial, but he pulled her around to face him

"Don't," he whispered and her denial died on her lips.

Her heart picked up its pace as her senses absorbed the man who stood before her. He smelled heavenly, his cologne a manly scent she couldn't even begin to decipher. His large hands were warm and strong against her arms and she longed suddenly to lean close to the broad chest that filled her vision. She lifted her face to him and her breath stopped at the look in his dark eyes. She had only a moment to take in the rugged handsomeness of his face before he bent his head and claimed her mouth in a kiss.

She fought valiantly for a minute, not wanting to give in to the mind-shattering passion that swirled between them. Then, with a quiet moan, the fight went out of her and she let herself go with it. He lifted his head, dark eyes searching her face. Running her fingers through his hair, she pulled his mouth down to hers again.

"Jenny," he whispered against her mouth and she shook her head.

She knew he still wanted to know the secrets and fears that made her push him away. However, all she wanted was more of the desire that filled them. This needed no explanation.

He pushed her away and looked down at her with eyes still dark with passion. She tried to step closer, but he held his hand up to stop her.

"Jenny, we can't do this," he said. "I can't do this."

"Why?" she whispered desperately.

"Because I really care for you. I've never felt the way I just did with anyone else. I've never felt the way I feel when I look at you with anyone else. I know we could have something really special, Jen, but only if you're willing to give up your secrets. Only if you're willing to trust me with yourself."

She started to speak and he held up his hand again.

"Your real self," he said firmly.

She looked at him for a long moment, fighting the emotions that filled her. Anger at him for not being willing to accept what she offered. Pain. And then, like a weed that refuses to die, hope. Hope that he would understand, hope that the police would catch the killer and she would be safe, hope that what he said was true and they really could have a life together.

Without a word, she led him to the other room, grabbed the yellowing newspapers from the bookshelf, and went to the front door.

"What the hell are you doing?" he said softly, but she could tell by the tone of his voice he knew she was showing him out.

She was silent as he came toward her, the hurt in his eyes giving way to slow burning anger in his eyes. Silently, she handed him the newspapers.

"This is what you need to know," she said before closing the door behind him.

The ringing telephone jarred her awake and Jenny fumbled around on the nightstand for it.

"Hello?" she whispered, running a hand over her face.

"What is this, Jenn?" His voice was soft and husky.

"Nick?" she asked, her eyes focusing on the red numbers of the clock beside her bed.

Three a.m.

"What the hell is this?" he repeated, anger and concern filtering through the phone line.

"Nick," she began, but he cut her off.

"I'm coming over."

"No! You can't!" she cried.

"Please," he whispered, the concern in his voice melting her heart.

She knew he was worried about what the articles meant, but she still wasn't sure she was ready for him to know. She had been invisible for so long, hidden in the shadows, and forced to blend in with her surroundings. Was she brave enough to venture out in the open, to let him see her past and know who she was?

She still remembered those brief shining years she lived in the spotlight, when the world opened before her like an oyster and people surrounded her because of who she was and what she stood for. Then, as suddenly as it came, it was gone, and she was as alone as she'd ever been. She restructured herself into the woman she was today. She liked her life as that woman, and she wasn't quite certain that woman was ready to open the wounds of her past to a man, even one she knew she could love.

"Jenny?" Her name whispered through the phone line, and the hint of anguish in it made her decision for her.

"Okay," she heard herself say and hung up the phone, slightly dazed by her agreement.

Ten minutes later, she sat on the sofa in her living room waiting for his knock on the door. When it came, she walked slowly toward the door, bracing herself to face him now that he knew the truth. Well, not the whole truth. She had been careful not to give him any articles identifying her as the Butterfly Girl. This was the first time she could remember ever having a man interested in her just because he liked her. If Nick had ever seen her in the commercials, he hadn't mentioned it. She liked the feeling of knowing that it wasn't her looks or her semi-famous status that interested him. It was her, Jenny Lewis, he was interested in. Or at least the Jenny Lewis he knew.

She opened the door and he stepped inside. Without a word, he pulled her into his arms and crushed his mouth to hers in an earth-shattering kiss. He whispered her name as his arms tightened and her knees went weak from his onslaught. He lifted his head slowly, looking as dazed as she felt before his face cleared and he stepped away from her. Though she wanted to follow him across the small space, she kept her distance.

His mouth tightened, making her stomach clench with misgiving. Ellie was wrong. She never should have told him.

"Are you very angry?" she whispered.

"Yes," he growled.

"At me?" She hated the weak, pitiful tone of her voice.

He swung around, anger as deep and dark as midnight in his eyes.

"How could you think I would be mad at you?" he demanded.

She shrugged at the disbelief in his voice.

"I thought you might be angry I hadn't told you."

"I can't imagine that it's something you want to relive by telling everyone you meet."

"No, it isn't."

"You just told Ellie, too. That's what was wrong with her the other day. She had no idea either until recently, did she?"

She shook her head.

"So, why, after all the years you two have been friends, did you finally tell her? And why did you tell me?"

She looked away for a moment, searching for the words to tell him without telling him too much.

"Tell me, Jen," he demanded firmly as if sensing her hesitation.

She spoke quietly without looking toward him. She told him how she had been left for dead on the bank of the river. How someone had found her and called the police. He sat silently, listening to her story. She could feel his unwavering gaze on her face as she talked.

"Did they catch him?" he barked when she grew silent.

"No," she answered with a small shake of her head.

"So he could still be out there somewhere?" She thought she heard a trace of fear in his voice. "You're not just avoiding the past. You're afraid he'll come back."

"He is out there somewhere," she said matter-of-factly.

"How can you be so sure?"

"One of the detectives who investigated the case contacted me Friday."

"And?" he prodded.

"They've discovered a connection between my kidnapper and what they believe to be a serial killer. He's killed ten girls since two thousand and three."

He stared at her in horror.

"They think there's a very good chance he may come after me again," she told him, her eyes bleak with fear.

Nick was on his feet in an instant, panic and fury in every line of his body.

She went willingly when he pulled her to him, grateful to lean her head against his large chest. She could hear the frantic beat of his heart as she stood and somehow it comforted her to know how frightened he was for her.

"What are we going to do, Jen?" he whispered against her hair.

*We.* She closed her eyes and basked in that one word. She wasn't alone. She breathed a prayer of thanks as she pushed back and looked up at him.

"I have it on very good authority that I should be concentrating on life, not death. So, we are going to go about our business and act like I never heard from Sam Conrad."

"How do we do that?"

"Ask me out again, Nick," she said with what she hoped was an encouraging grin.

He swallowed hard and his eyes searched hers.

"Will you go out with me, Jenny?" he asked, and then added softly, "Please."

She touched his face gently, a small smile playing about her lips.

"Yes."

Their eyes met and they stared at each other in silence for a long moment before she broke the silence.

"You have to go, Nick. I don't want Ellie's boys to see you here in the wee hours of the morning. They might get the wrong idea."

He grinned and nodded. "I'm sure they would."

At the door, he stopped and looked at her. "Are you okay here by yourself?"

"I'm fine," she reassured him. "Ed and Ellie are right next door. And you're just a few blocks over. I'll call if I need you."

"I'll see you tomorrow," he whispered against her mouth as his lips grazed hers.

"Good night, Nick," she answered as he moved away.

"Lock it," he commanded as he stepped through the door.

"Yes, sir," she grinned.

# CHAPTER THIRTEEN

April 29, 2005
Ocala, Florida
Claudia, *Euptoieta Claudia*

Claudia Eckert raced the horse across the open field, her long tawny braid bouncing with each movement of the horse's body. As the horse came to a stop before him, she smiled and slid from its back, the sun glistening off her bronzed skin.

"He's gorgeous, isn't he?" she said, shielding her eyes against the sun as the ranch hand led the horse back into the barn.

"Yes, yes he is," he agreed, a lie, of course. He had hardly even noticed the beast. He was too busy watching her, imagining her taking her place in Vanessa's circle.

"I just might buy him," she said as tears filled her eyes. "I think Tom would be happy if I bought him."

"I'm sure he would," he assured her, laying a sympathetic hand on her arm.

The sadness etched into her face and deep into the catlike golden eyes were was the first thing that caught his attention. He had followed her for a few days, finally approaching her at a church social a few weeks ago.

He hadn't been certain when he met her whether there was a butterfly named Claudia, so he had raced back to his hotel, confirming that one existed. Like the woman, the butterfly was described as tawny. He could think of no better word.

She was a widow whose husband had died unexpectedly and she had decided to use his insurance benefits to make their lifelong dream of owning horses come true.

"I should probably go home and think about it, but I don't think I need to. Let me do all the paperwork and then we'll go to the Red Oak Inn to celebrate."

63

*He could tell she was missing her husband, wanting to share their dream with someone. It was the pleading, vulnerable look in her eye that made him agree. He wasn't ready to kill her yet, but he would oblige her nonetheless.*

*Just before dawn, his car pulled out of the narrow dirt road that led to the back of the far pasture of the horse farm. It had been a few days early, not quite the first of May, but he had done it anyway, dumping her body while the cream-colored gelding watched silently from afar.*

# CHAPTER FOURTEEN

Jenny stared in disgust at her own reflection. With a groan, she threw herself back on the bed.

"It really isn't all that bad, Jenny," Ellie encouraged from the chair she occupied in the corner.

"Shut up, El," Jenny moaned as Ellie laughed.

"What is so funny?" Jenny demanded, rolling onto one side to glare at her friend.

"You. A week ago, you traipsed all over town looking like a bag lady and thought nothing of it. Now, here you are, in a dress that actually almost fits and your hair nearly tamed, and you feel miserably inadequate."

"This is all your fault, you know. I was perfectly happy without dating. But you just couldn't leave well enough alone. You had to keep trying and trying until you finally found someone I just couldn't resist!"

"I'm good. What else can I say?" Ellie teased. "Now get up before he gets here."

"Don't forget he doesn't know anything about Butterfly Cosmetics."

"Okay, but I don't understand your obsession with keeping him from knowing."

"Just this once it's nice to know someone is seeing me instead of her and actually liking what they see."

"Okey-dokey, then," Ellie said drawing the words out and raising her eyebrows comically.

"All right, I know that sounded a little insane, but I'm feeling a little insane right now. Just go along with me. Please."

"You're going to have to tell him eventually," Ellie warned as the doorbell rang and they headed downstairs.

"I know. Just not now."

65

"Don't wait too long."

"I won't. You're the best friend in the world," Jenny hugged her tightly. "Thanks, El."

Jenny opened the door and Nick stepped inside.

"Hi, Ellie."

"Hey, Nick."

"Ready?" he asked, turning to Jenny.

She nodded and he looked back at Ellie.

"I'll have her back by curfew, Ma'am," he teased as he led Jenny to his truck.

In the soft glow of the flickering candles and white lights strung across the trees overhead, Nick watched her lips move to the song the musician was singing. Hidden away in the darkened corner of the tavern's walled garden, she seemed to have let go of the tight rein she usually had on herself. She was relaxed, smiling and, if he guessed correctly, just a bit giddy from her single glass of wine.

"This is great," she said, taking another sip of wine. Her lips glistened with moisture and he reached across the table to cup the back of her head with his hand. Pulling her toward him, he kissed her, a small triumphant smile curving his mouth at her soft sigh.

She was blushing when she pulled away, a bemused smile dancing across her face.

"This is great," he said taking her hand and pulling her around the table to sit beside him on the bench.

He leaned back against the cool stone, and she let him bring her with him so that she rested against his side. It felt right for her to be there, close against him, her hair tickling his nose and her soft, sweet voice blending with the seductively mournful tone of the singer's.

"I had a wonderful time, Nick," Jenny said as he parked the truck in her driveway.

"Me, too," he murmured against her lips. His hand drifted through her hair, down her neck and held her captive as his gentle kisses followed its path. . He pulled back slowly, searching her face for her reaction. She stared up at him in breathless silence as he smiled slowly.

When they finally emerged from the truck, he caught her mouth again, kissing her thoroughly as she leaned back against the truck, pulling him snug against her.

Neither of them heard the car as it pulled into the yard next door.

"Way to go, Coach Jensen!" Kevin Pullman yelled out the car window as Derek Carson unfolded his long, lean body from the back seat.

Jerking apart, Jenny scrubbed her hand across her lips guiltily as Nick straightened to his formidable height. Then, meeting each other's embarrassed gaze, they burst into laughter and hurried toward her door.

"I don't think you should come in," she giggled.

"You're probably right. I guess we just gave them enough to talk about for now, huh?"

"Bye, Nick," she whispered, running a finger down his cheek.

He caught the finger with his lips, kissing it gently.

"I'll wait for your lights to come on upstairs. If I don't see them come on in a minute, I'm coming in. So, check everything out downstairs, and if everything's alright, turn the light on upstairs."

"What if something is wrong upstairs?"

He thought for a moment.

"Once you have the lights on, come to your window and wave at me if all's well. Then, I'll leave. Okay?"

"Okay."

He was walking away when she called his name.

"Thank you," she said and he knew instinctively that she was thanking him for wanting to make sure she was safe before he left.

"Good night, Jen," he said loud enough for the kids in the next yard to hear.

Milton bounded into the foyer to meet her as she locked the door, following obediently while she made her way through the house.

She flipped on her bedroom light before walking to the window. The moon illuminated the drive and she could see Nick leaning against the front of his truck, legs crossed at the ankles as he stared up at her window. Their eyes met, and even in the darkness, the attraction was like a magnet that pulled her toward him. She placed her palm flat against the window, wishing she could touch him once more. Disappointment rolled through her as he lifted his hand in a farewell salute, got into his truck and drove away.

Milt trailed her like a silent angry shadow as she got ready for bed. When she crawled into bed, her mind racing with thoughts of Nick and the night they had spent together, Milton lay on the floor beside the bed, staring at her with huge reproachful eyes.

"Oh, good grief, Milt, quit looking at me like that. I still love you." She reached down and scratched his ears affectionately. "But I think I've fallen hard for Nick Jensen."

# CHAPTER FIFTEEN

"I hear you and Coach Jensen have been seeing each other every night for the last two weeks," Anne Davis said in a slightly injured tone as she took the chair opposite Jenny's desk. "You didn't think that was something I'd like to know?"

"Where in the world did you hear that?" Jenny asked, looking up from the papers strewn across her desk.

"From the student grapevine. Is it true?"

Jenny sighed. There was nothing quite like the student grapevine to spread rumors at record speed. Except, of course, the faculty grapevine. There wasn't a doubt in her mind that everyone in the school knew by now.

"Yes, it's true."

"Wow! He's a really good-looking man. I can't believe –" Anne cut the rest of her observation off as Jenny looked at her sharply.

"That he likes me, right?"

"No," Anne denied quickly, but Jenny recognized the lie for what it was and gave Anne an understanding smile.

"Honestly, I wonder the same thing. I mean, look at me."

Anne looked for a long moment.

"Maybe he sees something else when he looks at you," she said and Jenny had the impression the woman was still searching her appearance for one redeeming quality.

"I guess," Jenny shrugged and went back to grading papers. She didn't need this right now. She asked herself the same questions every day. What was Nick doing with her? What did he see in her? She certainly didn't need someone who she had thought of as a friend to come in asking the same hateful questions.

"Well, I guess I'll go," Anne said, rising from the chair.

When she was alone again, Jenny laid her head on her arms. She and Nick had known it would happen eventually, but she had hoped to have a little bit of time before they became the talk of the teacher's lounge. They had forgotten teachers were the favorite fodder for the student rumor mill.

"What's up, Sweetheart?" Nick asked as he came into the room.

She looked up, surprised that he was here.

"Anne Davis just left. She heard we were dating and wanted to know if it was true."

"Yeah, I figured as much. Jeff Lipton just left my office. He wanted to know the same thing."

Jenny laughed softly, shaking her head in disbelief.

"So, we're the talk of the town, huh?"

"Looks like it," he agreed with a feigned grimace.

"So come over here and let's give her something to talk about, should she come back in." She wiggled her finger toward him. "I give her just about three seconds."

He chuckled and came around the desk, pinning her to the chair with his kiss.

"Jenny," Anne threw the door open. Her eyes widened in surprise. "Oops."

They laughed as she backed out of the room, her naturally pinched face bright pink.

"You think that worked?" he laughed against her mouth.

"I think that did the trick," she giggled. "I hope we don't get fired."

He chuckled, but backed up and sat down.

"Does the school have rules about teachers dating?" he asked.

"I don't know. When I read the manual, I skipped the parts I didn't think would apply to me."

"I guess we'll find out the hard way," he teased.

"Yeah, I guess so," she agreed, feeling suddenly out of sorts. She couldn't pretend it didn't bother her that people were talking about them. Especially since she knew everyone was asking the same thing. What was a gorgeous man like Nick doing with a mouse like her?

70

"What's the matter?" he asked, eyeing her with suspicion.

She shrugged as she busily straightened her desk.

He laid his hand on hers, holding them still.

"Tell me."

She felt the tears of humiliation gather in her eyes as she bowed her head.

"They all want to know what you're doing with me."

"What?"

"Everyone wonders why such a handsome, nice guy like you would even look twice at a woman like me."

Anger flashed in his eyes as she spoke.

"Anne said that?"

"Not in so many words, but she thought it as loudly as possible."

He laughed harshly.

"Anne Davis has asked me out no less than ten times, and I've declined each and every time. I'd say she's just angry."

"But I wonder the same thing," Jenny said quietly.

"Jenny, listen. I've told you before, you are a beautiful woman. I watch you with that mongrel of yours, with Ellie and her family, and with the kids here at school. You're warm and sweet and I can't resist you."

"You make me sound like a cinnamon bun," she grumbled.

"I like cinnamon buns," he replied, lifting his brows suggestively. "And anyone who doesn't must never have tasted one. They simply don't know what they're missing."

She laughed out loud.

"Now, come one. Let's go." He stood up and waited for her to come around the desk. Once she was beside him, he kissed her quickly and followed her through the door. "I'll see you at dinner."

When he showed up on her doorstep two hours later, he carried a brightly colored invitation to his twin nieces' birthday party.

"Will you go with me?" he asked as he held it out to her.

Glittering fairy princesses decorated the front and it was obvious the girls had written their names inside. She smiled to herself as she saw the way they had written "To Uncle Nick" in squiggly manuscript letters on the outside of the envelope.

Did she dare take this step? What if his family hated her?

"Will your parents be there?" she asked.

"Parents, siblings, nieces, nephews, cousins, aunts, uncles, everyone I know will be there."

He laughed at her terrified expression.

"They'll love you, Jen."

"Your sister won't mind you bringing me?"

"No."

"Are you sure?"

He narrowed his eyes at her as he pulled his cell phone out of his pocket and dialed a number.

"Trish, I'm bringing someone to the party. Is that okay with you?" He rolled his eyes. "Yeah, it's a girl. Yeah, I think you could call her my girlfriend."

"Nick!" Jenny hissed, feeling heat rise up her neck to her face. He winked at her as his sister continued talking.

"Thanks, Sis, see you then. Love you, too."

Jenny stared at him in wonder. How would it feel to belong to someone other than herself? What was it like to be able to say "I love you" so casually to another person? She had never known that kind of closeness, not even with her parents. Certainly not with her parents. Nina had been the closest she had come to having it, but Nina had her own ghostly memories of her own children and Jenny had always known she was just a substitute for the young Jamaican children who had perished in a house fire some twenty-odd years ago.

"Yoo-hoo, Jen," he said, drawing her attention to him. "My sister doesn't mind. So, will you go?"

"Yes."

She wondered if she looked as surprised by the word as she felt. What in the world was she doing? She had no idea how to act around one big happy family. She didn't even know how to act around a small uncaring family. She could tell Nick loved his family, though, so it was best to get it over with before their relationship went any further. If his family hated her, it would be easier for her to leave now than later.

72

# CHAPTER SIXTEEN

"Genevieve, come here," Nina called from the back of the store.

Jenny looked up from the counter where she was attempting to balance Nina's accounts.

"Hold on, Nina," she called as she began to add the whole column of numbers over again.

"Now," Nina insisted.

With an exasperated sigh, Jenny stood up and went through the door leading to the back room.

"Try this on." Nina held out a fitted blouse made of the orange and gold material Jenny had been admiring a few days before.

"Why?"

"I want to make sure I have the sleeves right for a woman about your size."

"Oh, Nina, for goodness sake, couldn't this have waited until I was done with the books?"

"No, it couldn't. Now, try it on."

Jenny quickly took off her baggy t-shirt and slipped the blouse on.

Without thinking, she hummed in contentment as the coolness of the material caressed her skin softly as it fell across her shoulders and down the length of her arms. Her eyes drifted closed for a moment as she reveled in the luxury. It reminded her of the gentle touch of butterfly wings on her face, cooling her sun-warmed cheeks.

Nina chuckled and Jenny's eyes flew open. She pulled the blouse off and jabbed it at the older woman.

"Keep it," Nina said.

"I thought it belonged to someone."

"It belongs to you," Nina informed her.

"I won't wear it," she said, folding her arms over her chest. Something told her that blouse would open the door for Nick to realize who she was.

Nina looked at her as if she were a small rebellious child, before turning away.

"Fine," she said. "It is a beautiful piece. I will sell it I'm sure."

Although the older woman tried to hide it, Jenny saw the hurt in Nina's eyes.

"Fine. I'll wear it. I might as well try to look half decent when I go to his sister's house."

Nina's face lit up.

"You're going to meet his sister?" she asked, excitement tingeing her voice.

"I'm going to his nieces' birthday party, Nina. It's no big deal. So don't go making a wedding dress or anything."

"Will his parents be there?" Nina asked.

"Yes."

"And you are okay with that?" Nina asked, her head cocked to one side.

"Of course, I'm okay with it. I'm a grown woman, Nina. I'm sure I can handle meeting his parents."

Nina shrugged eloquently.

"Of course," she agreed and turned back toward her sewing machine.

Realizing she had been dismissed, Jenny slid her t-shirt over her head and went back to the account books.

She stared at the numbers until they became a blur before her eyes and she realized there was no way she could concentrate. Contrary to what she'd told Nina, she was a nervous wreck about meeting Nick's parents. She hadn't been able to sleep since she told him she would go to the party with him. She had picked up the phone a dozen times to tell him she'd changed her mind. So far, she hadn't dialed his number.

"Quit biting your nails, Genevieve," Nina ordered sharply from beside her.

Jenny guiltily jerked her finger away from her mouth.

"Sorry," she murmured.

"You'll do fine, child." Nina patted her hand.

"Don't you have any words of wisdom or advice to offer me?" Jenny asked sarcastically.

"Just be yourself." Nina shrugged.

Jenny dropped her head into her arms, which were folded on the counter.

"Why does everyone tell me that?" she cried, her voice muffled.

She felt another of Nina's eloquent shrugs beside her.

"I'm leaving," she said impatiently and slammed the books shut. Jabbing them into the drawer under the counter, she grabbed her purse and headed for the door.

"Genevieve!" Nina called as she pushed the door open.

Jenny swung around just in time to catch the orange shirt the woman had tossed at her.

"Wear it," Nina ordered and disappeared into the other room.

# CHAPTER SEVENTEEN

Nick stared blankly at the woman who stepped out of Jenny's house dressed in blue jeans and a dark orange silk blouse. That's what she was hiding under her baggy skirts and long shirts? Why?

"Hey," she smiled self-consciously as he got out of the truck. He must have looked as stunned as he felt.

"Who are you?" he asked as he admired the shapely hips encased in her jeans.

"Is it that noticeable?"

She ran a hand over her hair in an attempt to calm it, the motion pulling the silk blouse tight against her full breasts. Desire thrummed through him, and he pulled her to him for a long, passionate kiss before answering.

"You look fine. More than fine, actually."

He studied her with a confused expression for a minute and then took her chin and made her look at him. "You didn't have to do this, Jenny. They would have loved you anyway."

"How do you know?"

"Because I loved you anyway."

She stared at him for a long moment, and then she shook her head in denial.

"Nick, you can't love me," she cried.

"Why not?" he demanded angrily.

"You don't know me," she cried.

"Yes, I do."

"No, you don't. Not really."

"And why is that, Jen?" he asked his eyes meeting hers.

She grew silent, knowing the answer he was demanding she give and knowing the truth of it.

"Because I won't let you," she whispered.

"Then let me know you. Let me love you. Not just the small part of yourself you've shown me, but all of you. I want to know and love all of you."

"I'm scared," she said truthfully.

"I know, Sweetheart, but I'm not going to hurt you."

"I know," she said, and in her heart she really did know, but in her head she was scared to death.

"Nick!" Patricia Benton cried as her younger brother came through the door. She rushed toward him and would have thrown her arms around him except for the birthday cake in one hand, the plastic spoons in the other, and the hugely pregnant belly that kept her from getting close enough.

"Hey, Trish." He kissed her on the cheek and rubbed her belly. "Is this the boy?"

"So they say," she laughed. "Mark's on cloud nine."

A gaggle of four-year-olds ran out of the dining room, across the foyer and through the living room. Obviously, the rooms were connected somewhere behind the staircase, because a few seconds later they reappeared, only to repeat the circle again.

Nick turned to Jenny, chuckling at the stunned look on her face.

"Trish, this is Jenny Lewis. Jen, this it my sister, Patricia."

"Trish," his sister laughed, "and you'll have to excuse the mess. And the noise."

Before Jenny could speak, Trish turned her head away and yelled, "Cake's ready!"

With her elbow, she ushered Jenny into the dining room where the children were jostling each other for room at the table.

"Uncle Nick!"

Two dark-headed girls darted past the other side of the table and launched themselves at Nick's legs, as Jenny watched in bemused silence.

"Monkeys!" Nick yelled bending to scoop the two tiny girls up into his arms.

"We aren't monkeys," one of them giggled.

"You're not?" he said in surprise. "Ooh, umm...what are you then?"

He looked totally confused and the girls giggled hysterically as he guessed.

"Puppies? Kitties? Llamas?"

"Uncle Nick," one of them said taking his face in her pudgy hands and looking him in the eyes, "you know we're girls."

"Girls? Yuck!" He loosened his grip, pretending he was going to let them fall, then caught them up again as they screeched with delight and grabbed him around the neck.

Jenny watched him, realizing with a small sigh, that this was a game he must play with them often. She had seen him with the kids at school. He was great with them, but seeing him with these two darling little girls laughing in his arms left her speechless.

"He's great with them, isn't he?" Trish whispered beside her.

Jenny blushed and looked away, knowing her feelings must have been showing on her face.

"Macy, Molly, are you going to blow out the candles on your cake?" Trish asked, walking around to her brother's side.

"We have to get down now, Uncle Nick," one of them told him in a serious voice.

He gave them each a kiss on their forehead and set them down. His eyes met hers over their heads and he winked, his mouth turning up in a knowing grin when heat bloomed on her cheeks and she glanced around self-consciously.

"Mom!" Trish called, "Are you coming?"

"Yes, Patricia. Hold your horses."

Trepidation made her heart skip a beat at the thought of Nick's mother coming into the room. She had never met a man's mother before. What was she supposed to say or do? What was expected of her? Her eyes shot toward the door. She could just slip out. She could wait in the car for Nick or she could catch a bus home or...

"Don't even think about it," he whispered in her ear.

She hadn't even realized he'd come to stand beside her, and it made her crazy that he could read her expressions so easily, as if her mind was an open book to him.

"I wasn't," she said with a last wistful look toward the door and a sigh.

"Here's the lighter, Patricia." Nick's mother came through the archway leading from the foyer, handed a pink lighter to her daughter and turned toward Nick.

"Hi, Sweetie." She beamed as Nick gave her an exuberant hug.

"Mark! Dad!" Patricia yelled.

"If that girl doesn't stop that yelling, I'm going to smack her," Nick's mother swore. "Did I yell like that?"

Nick began to nod, but stopped as his mother whacked him playfully on the arm.

"No, I did not, so don't you even say I did. She sounds like a fishwife for goodness sake."

Nick laughed and hugged his mother again. Jenny didn't think she'd ever seen people find such joy in each other's company. How could she, who had never had a real family moment, fit in around this bunch?

"Mom," Nick said, "I want you to meet someone."

For a moment, panic bubbled up, threatening to erupt. Then, his mother held her hand out, a welcoming smile on her face, and her eyes so much like Nick's that Jenny couldn't help but like her.

"Jenny, this is my mom, Barbara Jensen. Mom, this is Jenny Lewis."

"It's nice to meet you, Mrs. Jensen."

"Call me Barb. Only telemarketers call me Mrs. Jensen, and only my mother and really pushy telemarketers call me Barbara." As she spoke in her gruff, no nonsense way, Barbara Jensen ran her gaze over Jenny. Smiling in obvious approval, she patted Nick on the back in silent congratulations.

Then, waving at her husband who had just come into the room, she whispered loudly, "Donald, come meet Nick's girl."

"Jenny, this is Don, Nick's dad. Don, this is Jenny."

Jenny shook Donald Jensen's hand and looked up at Nick to see if it bothered him for her to be called his girl, but he just grinned and slipped an arm around her waist.

"We'll talk later," Barb promised as she was pulled closer to the table by the lit candles and giggling girls.

Jenny studied Barb and Don as they stood side-by-side taking pictures and talking to the birthday girls. They went together so

80

well, it was as if they had been cast in a part. Don was tall and broad-shouldered like Nick. But where Nick's hair was thick and dark, Don's was beginning to thin and turn gray. His eyes were blue, his smile easy and Jenny could picture younger versions of father and son playing catch on a warm spring day. Barb was short, but sturdily built. Her hair was a nicely dyed ash blond and cut short in an almost boyish style. Her dark brown eyes were accented by small laugh lines fanning out from the corners and deeper lines between her brows from squinting into the sunlight. She could imagine Barb in the stadium stands, wearing a football jersey and waving a flag as she cheered her son on. There wasn't a doubt in Jenny's mind that his family had supported Nick in everything he'd ever done.

Behind the Jensens was a man who could only be Nick's brother. It wasn't so much that he looked like Nick, although he did in some ways. It was more the way he held himself, the way he stood leaning against the archway with one foot crossed in front of the other. The way he seemed totally bored until you looked into his eyes. They were filled with the same warmth and easy acceptance that she had seen in the eyes of every one of the Jensens.

The whole room, adults and children alike, joined voices in an enthusiastic, if somewhat off key, rendition of the birthday song. As it concluded, the twins dove into their cake and their gifts with equal abandon.

"Those are from Jenny and me," Nick said as they pulled a pair of glittery lavender and pink bags close to them. "We couldn't agree on what to get you. You'll have to figure out which of us picked what."

The girls dug into the bags, throwing tissue paper out of the way.

"A baseball glove!" Macy exclaimed, holding it up for her mom to see.

Trish shook her head in exasperation at Mark's loud approval.

"A crown!" Molly cried as she put the rhinestone tiara on her head. "I'm a princess."

"Perfect!" Trish exclaimed with a smile of approval toward Jenny.

81

"I think your gifts were a hit," Barb said later at Jenny helped the ladies clean the kitchen.

Through the window, Jenny could see Nick playing catch with Molly and Macy. Both of them wore their tiaras and the lacy pink tutus they had retrieved from their playroom.

"So, you and Nick teach at the same school?" Trish asked as she wiped down the last section of counter and laid the dishcloth near the sink. "What do you teach?"

"English," Jenny said absently, barely able to pull her eyes away from Nick. As handsome as he was, today he was even more so, and as he threw his head back and laughed out loud at his niece's antics, she knew she was a goner.

"How long have y'all been dating?" Barb asked as she sat down at the small kitchen table.

"Three weeks," Jenny said, realizing how inadequate that sounded. Had it really only been a few weeks?

"But you've known each other longer, right?"

"We met the day he started coaching at the school."

"So you let your attraction simmer for the better part of a year and finally decided to turn up the heat?"

Jenny blushed, but met Barb's teasing grin with a smile of her own.

"Basically."

"Good, that's the best way. Make him have to think about it. What's wrong with women today is that too many of them are as sex-crazed as men and they jump in bed as soon as they see a halfway decent looking man. Now, my Nick, he's as cute as they come, but it darn sure won't hurt him for a woman to make him wait and work for her attention." Barb patted Jenny's hand reassuringly. "You did good."

Jenny started to tell the woman that it hadn't been intentional. She simply didn't know how to throw herself at a man and beg him for attention. Instead, she just smiled and pretended that playing hard to get had been her intention all along.

"Jen, are you ready to go? These two are wearing me out!" Nick stuck his head in the door.

"Nick, don't leave yet!" Trish protested. "It just got quiet in here. We ladies can finally settle down and talk."

"Now, I know it's time to go," he said with a grimace in his sister's direction, "Jenny doesn't need to be interrogated, and she certainly doesn't need to hear all those stories you're going to tell her about me."

"Go play, Nicholas," his mother ordered with a dismissive wave of her hand.

His eyes darted to Jenny as if assuring himself that she was okay. She gave him a slight nod and he smiled encouragingly back at her.

"Yes, ma'am, but only for a few more minutes. Then we really have to head back home." He disappeared again and a moment later, Jenny saw him through the window crawling around like a horse with one of the twins on his back and the other leading him around with imaginary reins.

"Where are you from, Jenny?" Barb asked.

"Orlando."

"And your parents live there?" Barb prodded, apparently unashamed of her unbridled curiosity.

"No, my parents live in Athens."

"Georgia?"

"Greece."

Barb's eyes widened and Jenny grinned at her.

"Greece?" Barb repeated and Jenny nodded. "They travel a lot and they have a condo down south, but Greece is the place they consider home."

"What do they do there?" Trish's eyes shone with interest.

"I have no idea. I've never visited them there."

"Do they work?" Barb asked.

"My father owns an art gallery. He also buys and sells antiquities. My mother does whatever she wants."

"Are they rich?" Trish asked, looking startled by the question. "Sorry."

Jenny shrugged nonchalantly. "I suppose they are."

"And yet you chose to become a teacher?"

"Yes."

"Why?"

She had chosen teaching because it seemed far away from the teenage sex symbol she had become as the Butterfly Girl. Long before her life had changed so dramatically, she had decided she wanted something different. But how did she explain this to the woman sitting before her? How could she explain it to them, when she hadn't even gotten up the nerve to tell Nick what she had been?

Barb and Trish were watching her closely, waiting for her response. Finally, she told them the truth about her family, even if not about herself.

"I know this is probably hard for someone from a family like yours to understand, but my parents and I have never been close. There was a time as a child I would have loved nothing more than to be like you all must have been. But even then, they were busy people. Too busy to be bothered with a child anyway. I love my parents; they are, after all, my parents and in their way, they love me. We see each other when we see each other and we're actually much closer now than we've ever been before or than I ever thought we could be. But their lifestyle seems rather boring and meaningless, to me. Teaching was the perfect alternative to that. There's never a dull moment, and no matter how thankless a job it can be, it is far from meaningless."

Barb patted her hand in approval and Trish looked at her with a mixture of sympathy and admiration.

"You'll get used to our nosiness, Jenny. That's one of the flaws of a close family. Everyone thinks they're entitled to know everything. If we get too personal, just tell us to butt

out," Barb advised with a grin. "We'll usually oblige."

"Okay, now, it's really time to go, Jenny. I need a nap," Nick said as he came into the kitchen, a girl wrapped around each leg. His hair stuck up on end, no doubt because it had been used as a bridle, and his shirt was wrinkled and dirty. And, at that very moment, with the two little girls, their tiaras askew on their dark heads, wrapped around his legs while he walked across the kitchen with them on his feet, Jenny knew for a fact that she was in love.

84

# CHAPTER EIGHTEEN

The phone was ringing as Jenny came through the door with Nick just behind her. The answering machine picked up before she could reach it, and Sam's booming voice came through.

"Genevieve, it's Sam. I need to talk to you, babe. Call me the minute you get in."

Babe? Jenny thought as Sam rattled off his cell phone number. Had he ever called her

sweetheart? In all the time she knew him, he had never uttered an endearment to her. Why now? Why with Nick standing right behind her? She turned, hoping Nick hadn't noticed. He looked like she had punched him in the stomach. Shock, hurt, and a million questions blazed to life in his eyes.

"Nick, that wasn't what you're thinking," she said quickly, defensively.

"What is it then?"

"Sam's the detective who handled my case. He's been my only contact with the police in Brevard County since I moved to St. Augustine." She tried to explain, knowing that the endearment and the familiarity in Sam's tone made her explanation ring false.

Suddenly, without warning, Nick pulled her roughly into his arms and crushed his mouth to hers. This was like no kiss she'd ever known. There was no sharing, no tentative exploring of each other. There was only Nick taking and demanding and then, with a groan, pushing her away.

"Nick," she pleaded as he turned back toward the door. "Nick, I swear it isn't like that between Sam and me. It never was."

"How was it then?" he demanded angrily.

She hesitated a moment, then her hazel eyes filled with tears and regret, and she looked away.

"I never loved him," she whispered.

"But you had a relationship with him, didn't you?"

"Yes." Her voice trembled as she stared out of the dining room window into the darkness.

"And do you still?"

"No! Nick! Please," she beseeched him to believe her. "He was the only person I knew. Neither of us ever wanted any more out of it than what we got."

He took a ragged breath and cupped her cheek with his hand.

"I don't want to lose you, Jenny," he said quietly as he laid his forehead against hers.

"You're not going to lose me, Nick," she whispered huskily. It was as close as she could come to revealing the truth of her feelings for him.

"You need to call him, don't you?" he asked as if sensing her need to know what the cop had to tell her. He smiled a little as she nodded and then with a kiss on her forehead, he backed away.

"Sam?" She gripped the phone so tightly her knuckles turned white. Anguish thickened her voice. "Oh, no. When? Where?"

Concerned by the increasing pallor of her face, Nick moved to her, wrapping his arms around her from behind. He could feel her trembling as she leaned into him. When Sam continued to talk and she began to cry in earnest, Nick could stand no more. He grabbed the phone from her, interrupting the man on the other end.

"She'll call you back tomorrow," he growled into the receiver as Jenny turned into his arms. Sam was yelling on the other end as Nick placed it into the cradle.

"He'll be furious," she hiccupped against his chest.

"I don't care," Nick informed her, itching for a reason to plow his fist into the unknown man's face.

Without letting her go, he walked to the sofa and pulled her down beside him. Sensing she needed a few moments to compose herself, he remained silent as she buried her face in his neck and cried. When she finally spoke, the words froze his breath in his chest.

"He killed another girl," she sobbed. "She was only eighteen years old."

86

Nick's arms tightened around her as he closed his eyes and kissed the top of her head gently.

"I'm so sorry, Jenny," he mumbled against her hair.

"He left a note. He left another note." Her sobs made her words hard for him to understand.

"What did it say?"

She sobbed harder as she shook her head wildly.

Realizing she was refusing to tell him, he pushed her back and looked into her anguished eyes.

"What did it say?" he demanded again.

"It said he's coming back for me."

"So what is your friend, Sam, doing to protect you?"

"There's nothing he can do to protect me. No one can protect me."

She sounded so resigned to such a horrible fate that he shook her a little.

"No one's going to hurt you," he insisted, desperation making his voice harsh. "I'll protect you, even if he can't."

She saw the determination in his eyes, the feeling behind his vow, and she knew he meant what he said. She couldn't bring herself to tell him again that there was no hope. She was as good as dead, and there was nothing they could do about it. She didn't say that the killer had demanded she reappear in two weeks, and that she intended to do exactly what the police and the killer wanted. She would become the Butterfly Girl once more, and she would willingly walk into his trap, but she would do it in her own time. She wouldn't do this one moment earlier than she absolutely had to. She knew in her heart he wouldn't take her until she had, once again, changed from a caterpillar into a butterfly. So, she would put the fateful makeover off as long as she could. She had two weeks, fourteen days. When those days were over, she would step into a salon as Jenny Lewis, schoolteacher, and reemerge as Genevieve Lewiston, Butterfly Girl. She refused to give him one extra day.

What would Nick say if she told him who she was right now? She was absolutely sure he cared for her, not based on her looks, not based on her parents' money, but because of her. Would he feel the same way when he realized she had lied to him? Would he forgive her? She quickly decided not to take that chance. He would find out when it was over. Then, she supposed it wouldn't matter to her one way or the other.

She would be dead.

*He sat on the bank of Mantanzas Bay, twirling the long pin holding the brown and orange butterfly between his fingers. Very soon now, the junonea genoveva would be where she belonged and the collection would be complete. It was time to bring it all to an end.*

*He had made sure there were butterflies in heaven, each and every one of them sent there for Vanessa as tokens of his love. Now it was time for him to join her.*

*He felt his heart swell with happiness. Genevieve was still the most perfect specimen he had ever found. Not only did she share the name of the butterfly, she was the Butterfly Girl.*

*Vanessa loved Butterfly Cosmetics, and he'd bought her something from them on every special occasion they shared. It was only fitting that for their reunion, the most special of occasions, he gave her this most precious gift.*

*His hand stilled and he stared at the butterfly for a long, silent moment. He could still hear Vanessa's voice reading the description of the tropical buckeye to him, how the huge orange spots at the bottom of its wings helped protect it from predators. It reminded him of Genevieve in that way too.*

*Her eyes haunted him nearly as often as Vanessa's large dark gaze did. It would be difficult to kill her when he knew the woman behind that turquoise gaze.*

*With a sigh, he carefully placed the butterfly specimen back in its package. He had held onto it for many years now, waiting for the time to recapture the one that got away.*

88

# CHAPTER NINETEEN

Jenny spread the contents of the portfolio across the coffee table. A younger, much more glamorous version of herself smiled back at her. The face, the smile, the unadulterated joy and excitement shining in her eyes: all had served to win her a place with Butterfly Cosmetics.

Butterfly catered to teenage girls and young women and she was the perfect face for their campaign. Their business was based on enhancing natural beauty. In their earlier commercials, they had shown before and after pictures of teenage girls who used the makeup. A parade of them had come and gone, smiling for the pictures, then disappearing once again into the world of everyday teenagers. She had been different.

From the very first commercial she had appeared in, Butterfly's sales had improved. Cannon Brockway had commanded that his advertising department come up with a campaign featuring her alone, and within a few months, she was being recognized on the street.

For the six years she was the Butterfly Girl, their sales had steadily improved, and she'd had other companies approach her, knowing she would soon outgrow the beautifully innocent Butterfly commercials. They were cosmetic companies catering to women who saw her blossoming maturity as the stroke of good fortune they were looking for. Jenny's natural beauty was the perfect face for a generation of woman who sought a more natural beauty than the one before.

Genevieve smiled now at the irony of the fact that although she had become a sort of icon to teenagers, she barely had any experience with people her own age. Although she had acquaintances of all ages, the only real friends she had were Suzy Prather, whom she'd gone to boarding school with, and Patty

Jenkins, a fellow model. All three of them had turned twenty-two the year she was abducted, but truthfully, she had always felt years older than either of them. While she spent her afternoons on photo shoots and commercial work, they went to the mall, rollerbladed and chilled out in front of the television. She was representing Butterfly Cosmetics at various functions while they spent their weekends partying and chasing boys.

While she enjoyed her role as the Butterfly Girl, she had been sure she didn't want to pursue that sort of work with any other company. She was already making plans to leave after graduation.

Until that fateful night, she had only been to one party, other than company Christmas parties and the occasional birthday party for someone at Butterfly. The other girls insisted she not miss every party in college. So, with some trepidation, she agreed to attend the last party of the year. She had to admit she'd felt as if she was on the verge of an exciting new adventure as she climbed out of the car with her friends and entered the smoky, booze-scented fraternity house with Suzy and Patty at her side.

Of course, it hadn't taken her long to remember why she didn't go to parties, so she was actually relieved when Evan called to tell her Cannon wanted to see her immediately.

For the past six years, she'd wondered what her life would be like if she'd refused his summons.

"Why is this door unlocked?" Nick's voice interrupted her reverie.

With a startled gasp, she quickly stuffed the pictures back into the folder shoved them under the sofa as Nick came through the door.

"I guess I forgot to lock it after I took Milt out this morning."

"Don't forget again," he scolded as he dropped her mail on the table and bent to kiss her.

She picked up the stack of mail and began sorting through it. She stopped as she

came to the lavender linen envelope with her name and address written in her mother's familiar penmanship.

She groaned as she stared at it.

90

"What?" Nick's voice was sharp with concern.

"It's from my mother," she held the envelope up as dread lodged in her stomach.

"Well, aren't you going to open it?" he asked, obviously not understanding why she was upset.

Her hands shook a little as she opened it. Somehow, she knew this was not going to be something she liked. If anyone could destroy the little bit of time she had left with the man she loved, it was Helene Lewiston.

She didn't have to read far to know exactly how it would happen. Her parents were in Florida for her father's sixtieth birthday, and her mother was planning an outrageously overboard party to celebrate. If Jenny could, she would refuse to go, but this party would be her last chance to see her parents. She had to go, even if it was only to say good-bye.

Nick ran a gentle hand down her back, as if he could sense her dismay. What was she going to do about him? Would he hate her when he learned what a huge part of her life she'd kept hidden from him? Would she lose the last few precious days she had with him? Would she lose him completely?

She took a shuddering breath, fighting back the panic her mother's letter caused, and turned to look at him.

"Are you okay?" he asked, his eyes burning into hers as if searching for answers.

"I, um, I don't know."

"You don't know if you're okay?" he asked, a teasing light in his eyes. "Your mom must be something else."

She managed a halfhearted smile, and shook her head.

"My mom is something else, and she's having a huge party Saturday."

"And this upsets you, why?"

"I need a makeover," she blurted out before she could stop herself from saying the words.

"Is that what this is all about?" he exclaimed in bewilderment. "A makeover?"

She nodded silently. It wasn't as if she were really lying. The makeover was the problem.

91

"So you don't want a makeover?"

"No."

"Then don't have one. They're your parents. They know what you look like. Why do you want to change that?" He looked so endearingly bewildered, she smiled and shrugged, trying to smooth over her initial panic.

"I haven't seen my parents in three years. I want to look my best. Believe it or not, this is not my best."

"Okay," he shrugged in a sort of agreement. "You're in luck. Trish is a beautician. That's what she did before she had the twins. Why don't we go over and get her to work her magic?"

"Not until Saturday," she cried. Then with what she hoped was a reassuring smile, "We'll make a special night out of it. We can surprise each other with how great we look all dressed up."

"It's a date," he grinned.

"Call Trish and make sure she can help. If not, I'll need to make an appointment somewhere." Jenny prayed that Nick's sister would do it. She needed to witness her metamorphosis away from prying eyes and any more witnesses than absolutely necessary.

Once Nick left, Jenny picked up the phone to call Sam. She felt slightly guilty for waiting for Nick to leave, like she was hiding something from him. But she hadn't wanted to have to explain to him why she needed to call Sam. Which she guessed, proved she was hiding something, but it was something she just couldn't bring herself to tell him. Truthfully, she didn't know how to tell him now. There had been too many opportunities for her to say something, too many times when she should have told him. Now, she had no choice but the only way she could bear for him to learn the truth was for her to simply make the transformation and face the consequences.

Sam picked up on the first ring and Jenny quickly told him about her father's birthday party.

"So, I guess I'll be turning back into myself on Saturday," she said trying to sound calm.

"That doesn't give us much time, Gen," he said, sounding slightly disgruntled.

"I know, Sam, but I have to go." Her voice broke and she paused for a moment before she went on. "This is the last time I'll be seeing them."

He swore viciously.

"Can't you give us a little credit, Genevieve? We're going to do our best to protect you and catch him."

"I'm sorry. I know you'll try. But I'm scared, Sam. I'm really, really scared."

"Listen, Sweetheart. It won't be as bad this time. Honestly, it won't. You'll know what to expect. You won't be caught totally off guard."

She closed her eyes and leaned her head back on the sofa. How could it be better to know she was going to die than to simply die without warning?

"I'm sure he won't hit on Saturday. After all, he won't realize the transformation has taken place until he sees pictures of you. We'll have to make sure pictures get to the papers, along with a statement about you being the Butterfly Girl when you were young. Then, after the party, we'll set up security around your house and around the school. We'll get this guy before he gets to you."

Trying to sound reassured and praying Sam was right, Jenny agreed it was a good plan, said good night and hung up. As she lay down that night, she wondered if she would live to know the feeling of being wrapped in someone's arms while she slept or the feeling of having someone there when she woke up. She thought of Nick and how nice it would be to open her eyes to his handsome face every day for the rest of her life. Then, remembering that the rest of her life may only be the next week, she closed her eyes and prayed it wasn't.


"What am I going to do, Nina?" Jenny moaned as she sat at the tiny table in Nina's workroom.

"You're going to do what you need to do," the older woman said as her fingers worked the needle quickly in and out of the golden material she worked on.

"But, Nina, what if they don't catch him in time? What if I die this time?" Fear rose in her throat like bile as she thought of the

93

ribbon cutting into her wrists and ankles, the suffocating weight of the plastic.

Nina's eyes shot from the material she worked on, meeting Jenny's sternly.

"Life is full of 'what ifs', Genevieve. Each morning, we face the day without knowing where our lives will go before nightfall. Each night, we lay our heads down trusting we will wake to see another day. No one—not one single person— knows what the future has in store for them. We must simply have faith and believe that all will work out the way it is meant to. And we must do our best to face the end with no regrets."

As she finished speaking, Nina's eyes lowered to her sewing. She had spoken little of her life before she had come to live with the Lewiston family. Jenny knew that she had been married and had children who had died, but that was it. Those were the only details she had ever been given.

"Do you have regrets?" Jenny whispered now.

"Oh, yes, Genevieve, I have regrets."

She lifted her face, staring sightlessly toward her shop, lost in the distant past with the memories that haunted her.

"Once, long ago, I lived without taking chances. I lived in fear and uncertainty, afraid to let my babies out of the house. Afraid of the things that would befall them if I didn't watch them every moment. We lived far from the nearest town, Leon and I. We had moved out into the forest with his family. We had two beautiful girls, Ana and Mara. They were smart, sweet little girls. I had seen people lose their children. Seen them die from snakebites and diseases. Seen them lost in the quick moving river that flowed between our village and the nearest town. I was determined that nothing like that would befall my girls. So, as they grew, Leon and I found different ways to keep them in the house. Not always. When I could dedicate my complete attention to them, I took them outside to play in the sunshine. But our life was hard; we didn't have the conveniences offered to us here in this country and there were many times that my entire day was spent outside working. The children were two and three when I convinced Leon to build the girls a small pen inside the house."

94

Her lips trembled and her dark eyes shone with the guilt and pain she had hidden for so long. A soft sob escaped her and she lowered her gaze to her lap as she seemed to battle for control of her emotions.

"I caged my babies, Genevieve. And when the fire came, they couldn't escape. I was down by the river with the laundry; sure they were safe and sound in our little home. All the other children played in a small clearing between the village and the river. I wondered how the mothers could stand to turn their backs away for a moment. I was smug in my knowledge that no ill could befall my children. Leon and I had made sure they were safe."

Tears rolled down her wrinkled cheeks. "I smelled the smoke at the same time that one of the other women cried out. I turned to where she pointed and saw my house burning. I ran as fast and as hard as I could to get there, but it was too late. I heard their cries all the way up the path. But as one of Leon's brothers grabbed me and kept me from rushing into the fire, their desperate cries were replaced by silence. Their pain was over in just a few minutes, but mine has lasted forever."

Nina quickly rubbed her hand across her eyes and sighed. But still, she didn't raise her face to Jenny's.

"So, you see, child, no matter how hard we try to control fate or the hand of God, or whatever you choose to call it, we are powerless to change what will be. All we can do is live with what has passed and learn whatever we were meant to learn from the experience."

"What could you possibly have learned from that, Nina?" Jenny's voice broke with sympathy.

Nina lifted her face and aimed a sad, wise smile at Jenny.

"I learned that we cannot cage the people we love. No matter how much we love them, or how great our fear of losing them, it is our duty to encourage them to step out in faith and hope. It is the only way they will ever learn to live."

Jenny swiped at the tears that streamed from her eyes.

"How much would my girls have learned about the world caged up like little animals? How strong would their bones and muscles have been? I let my fear control me, child. And it cost me

95

my babies. I don't want to see you let your fear cost you what your heart holds dear."

Nina pushed herself slowly to her feet. Jenny noticed how small and tired she suddenly seemed as she made her way to the closet on the far side of the room. With hands trembling slightly, Nina reached into the recesses of the closet.

"This is yours, my Genevieve" she said as she turned.

"Oh, Nina," Jenny breathed as she studied the beautiful turquoise dress Nina held up for her inspection. "How did you know I would need it?"

She knew her mother had told Nina about the party, but that hadn't been a guarantee that Jenny would agree to wear something so glamorous.

"Remember the day the material came? Your young man came in carrying the box. He couldn't keep his eyes off of you. And, although you were not as obvious, you couldn't keep yours off of him either. I knew when you pulled it out of the box exactly was I was going to do with it. And I knew you would wear it one day."

Jenny smiled as she remembered that day and Nina's cryptic assurance that the material would be perfect.

"Thank you," she whispered and wrapped her arms around the older woman's neck.

"You just remember what I said, child. You make peace with the past and live the life God has blessed you with at this moment. That's all any of us are doing."

# CHAPTER TWENTY

"Trish!" Nick yelled as he opened her front door. "I brought your next victim."

"Very funny, Little Brother," Trish said from the top of the stairs. Then, to Jenny, who had just elbowed him in the ribs, "I'll be right there. I'm attempting to get these two monkeys down for a nap. If I'm not down in a minute or two, it means they won and I fell asleep before they did. Just come get me. You can hang your dress up on the coat rack behind you."

She turned away, her stomach looking twice as big as it had last week.

"Are you sure she doesn't mind doing this? She looks awfully..." Jenny trailed off, not wanting to say anything that might offend Nick or Trish.

"Pregnant?" he supplied with a teasing grin. "I think the word is pregnant."

"Are you talking about me?" Trish demanded from the stairway.

"Actually, Jenny was just saying you looked awfully pregnant," Nick said, inclining his head toward Jenny who could feel her face turning red with embarrassment.

"Nick!" she exclaimed.

"It's okay," Trish said, shooting her brother a quelling look as she patted her tummy. "I am awfully pregnant."

"That was fast," Nick commented, craning his head toward the stairs.

"I bribed them with a video. They can watch it for the hundredth time as long as they are lying down and being quiet. They'll be asleep in a few minutes."

"Good thinking." Nick started toward the door. "Are you sure you two are going to be okay?"

"Yes," both women said at the same time.

When he was gone, Trish turned to Jenny.

"So, how do you want to look?"

"You're the professional. You decide how you think I should look. I'll agree to anything." Jenny assured her.

Trish lifted a strand of Jenny's frizzy, blond hair in her hand.

"What color is this naturally?" she asked.

Jenny took a deep breath before answering. She realized with heart-lurching certainty that once she started down this path, there was no turning back.

"Red," she said quietly and Trish nodded her head.

"That's what I thought. With your coloring, that's the only color it could be. C'mon into the kitchen. I've got everything set up in there."

"It won't hurt the baby for you to be around the hair dye, will it?" Jenny asked in concern.

"No, but if it'll make you feel better, I'll let you do it and I'll hold my breath so I don't inhale the fumes."

Jenny laughed as she followed the woman into the kitchen.

Three hours later, the two women had moved to Trish and Mark's room where Trish was busily applying the finishing touches to Jenny's makeup. With a theatrical flourish of the powder brush, she stepped back to survey her handiwork.

"Oh, my God," she breathed as she took in the whole effect of the makeup and hair together. She silently turned the chair Jenny sat in so that it faced the mirror.

Jenny wasn't sure whether to be happy or horrified by the image she saw there. The shoulder length auburn hair, layered around her face and curling toward her chin, the startling blue-green eyes lightly lined and shadowed with brown, the coral lips and flawless skin.

With every snip, splash and brush, Trish had coaxed out those traits that once made her the Butterfly Girl, all those traits that now made her a target. She lifted her eyes to meet the stunned brown ones of the woman behind her.

"You're really good, Trish," she said quietly.

"Does Nick know who you are?" Trish asked still staring at Jenny in shock.

Jenny shook her head.

"I didn't want him to know. It was so nice to be anonymous. To know he liked me."

Trish nodded, looking as if she were trying to understand.

"He was obsessed with you," she chuckled.

Jenny's eyes widened as a jolt of fear swept through her. "He was what?"

"Obsessed with you. When you first became the Butterfly Girl. Gosh, he must have been about sixteen, and he thought you were the most beautiful girl on earth. I suppose most of the boys in America thought the same thing." Trish laughed. "He's going to have a cow."

Jenny tried to calm her racing heart. Of course, Trish hadn't meant he was obsessed like some kind of psychopathic stalker. It was just a figure of speech. Besides, Nick could never be the killer. In her heart, she knew that. In her mind, though, she knew everyone would be suspect tonight.

"Get dressed," Trish commanded, laying the garment bag containing Jenny's dress on the bed. "I'm going downstairs to make sure there isn't anything sticky and gooey on the kids, the walls, or the floors before you come down. I don't want you to ruin your dress. I'll let you know when Nick gets here."

Trish started out of the room, and then turned to look once more at Jenny.

"You look gorgeous, Jenny," she said as their eyes met in the mirror. "When he sees you, Nick will forget all about being mad that you didn't tell him."

Jenny smiled at the reassurance, but doubted it was going to be that simple with Nick.

Once she was alone, she studied herself in the mirror. She had hoped in vain that she had changed so much that the killer would no longer want her. But as she regarded her reflection, she knew that she hadn't gotten her wish. She may look a little older, but, all in all, the same face stared back at her now as six years ago.

Before she could succumb to the fear at the back her mind, She heard Nick's voice downstairs and realized she was still sitting in the same spot Trish had left her. And she was still dressed only in her undergarments. She quickly got up and unzipped the garment bag. Soft turquoise silk washed over her, hugging her breasts and waist, before flowing loosely to her ankles.

"Nick's here," Trish announced before stepping into the room. For a second, she just stared at the vision she had helped create. "He's going to be so surprised."

Jenny thought that was probably the understatement of the year. But she kept the thought to herself as she slipped her matching shoes on and reached for the chiffon wrap she used to cover her bare shoulders. The wrap was the finishing touch. It was almost transparent turquoise covered with butterflies that had been embroidered with silver thread.

Taking a deep breath, Jenny tried to smile without showing her apprehension.

"It's go time," she murmured as Trish nodded an acknowledgement and hurried to get Nick.

Nick watched in open-mouthed surprise as the beautiful turquoise-swathed woman came down the steps. She looked nothing like the woman he'd left in his sister's care this morning. Nothing like the woman he had fallen in love with.

"What do you think?" Trish asked excitedly from his side.

"I think she's beautiful. But she isn't Jenny. Not my Jenny."

"Nick, don't be an ass. Of course, she's Jenny. And she's beautiful. Is that so horrible?"

"What in heaven's name did you do to her?" he growled.

"Nick," Trish scolded.

Jenny stopped her descent and stood on the stairs, wide, hurt eyes boring into him. For a moment, he wanted nothing more than to beg for her forgiveness for his careless words, but then, just as suddenly, betrayal washed over him as he realized what she had kept from him. He swore softly and walked into the dining room.

Jenny cursed herself silently as he turned away. She had known it, known all along how hurt and angry he would be, but she had played her stupid game anyway. She'd done it all to prove that someone could love her who had no idea who she was, to prove there was someone out there who could love Jenny instead of the Butterfly Girl.

She staggered down the steps, her heart breaking in her chest as she realized she had found him, found the one and only man who would love the woman she had become and now she may have lost him.

Trish put an arm around Jenny's hunched shoulders as she stepped off the last step. She wanted nothing more than to cry her eyes out on her new friend's shoulder. But even as she longed to give in to her tears, she knew she had a job to do. She had to show up tonight as the beautiful butterfly. It was the only chance they had to ever catch the killer.

Pushing herself out of Trish's comforting embrace, Jenny turned toward the dining room. Nick sat at the table, his face covered with his hands as she entered. She made her way toward him and laid her hand on his shoulder.

"Nick," she whispered in supplication as he lifted his head and stared at her.

"Why, Jen? Why didn't you tell me?" he whispered.

"I couldn't, Nick. I just couldn't." Her voice broke and she bit her lip to keep it from trembling.

"Why not?" his voice was thick with betrayal and pain.

"I was frightened."

"Of me?"

"No, of everything. I was afraid of being loved because of who I was. I was afraid he would find me. I was so very, very afraid, that I would lose you."

"Why did you do this now?" he asked, searching her face for some explanation.

She couldn't look at him and speak the lie that came from her lips.

"I couldn't disgrace my parents by going to the party looking like I usually do. My mother would be furious, not to mention hurt. Besides, I haven't seen them in years and I want to look my best."

"But won't this call more attention to you?" he whispered in horror.

She nodded and panic filled her as she thought of what she would be doing tonight.

He pulled her close as if sensing her fear and whispered quietly in her ear.

"I'll protect you, Sweetheart. You stay close to me and I won't let anyone get close enough to hurt you. No one outside your parents' party even has to know how you look tonight."

She felt her heart break at what would be the ultimate betrayal of his vow. He had forgiven her so easily. She felt certain his forgiveness wouldn't be so forthcoming in the morning.

# CHAPTER TWENTY-ONE

As they crossed the sparkling ballroom, Jenny drank in the sight of her parents. Her mother wore a sequined violet gown, and beneath her sleek silver bob, diamonds sparkled from her ears and neck. She wore a pair of matching shoes that made her a half-inch taller than her husband, who stood a few feet away talking with a familiar looking man. Her father wasn't a large man, but he had an air that, along with his gorgeous good looks, made him seem much larger than he was. His jet-black hair was turning white at the temples, but other than that, he didn't appear to have aged at all since she last saw him. His dark eyes danced with merriment as he turned away from the blond man he was talking to and toward them.

"Genevieve, my love," he cried and hurried toward her. "You look beautiful. You're mother will be overjoyed to see our beautiful girl has returned."

"Hello, Daddy," Jenny said as she kissed her father on the cheek.

"Helena, look who's arrived," he said as he led her toward her mother.

"Oh, darling!" Helena Lewiston exclaimed. She kissed the air beside Jenny's cheek and Jenny breathed in the exotic scent her mother of her mother's perfume.

Helena stepped back without letting her daughter's hand go and eyed Jenny appreciatively. "You look beautiful. I'm so glad you gave up that horribly pitiful way of dressing that you had the last time we saw you. You looked like a beggar, a very plain, fat beggar."

Jenny smiled wanly as her mother carried on about her clothes and hair.

"Did Nina make this gown?" she asked circling Jenny as she lifted the fabric in her hands. "It's absolutely gorgeous. "I swear that woman could make a fortune if she would let me tell my friends about her."

"Nina doesn't want to make a fortune, Mama. She likes it here and her shop is doing quite well," Jenny said, wishing her mother would accept that everyone wasn't like her.

Finally, as Helena's discourse wound down, Jenny pulled Nick up beside her.

"Mother, this is Nick Jensen. Nick, this is my mother, Helena Lewiston, and my father, Daniel."

"It's very nice to meet you, Mrs. Lewiston, Mr. Lewiston," Nick shook each hand in turn and Jenny smiled at the appreciative look on her mother's face.

Nick was ravishingly handsome tonight. The tuxedo seemed to make him look even more masculine than usual and the stark white of the shirt against his dark good looks was stunning.

"And what do you do, Mr. Jensen?" Helena asked, quickly disregarding his handsomeness for what she considered to be much more important.

Jenny rolled her eyes at her mother's usual prying. No matter that neither she nor her husband had ever had time for their daughter, they still felt it their duty and God-given right to make sure the people she associated with were up to par.

"I teach."

"Oh, how—well—how nice," Helena stammered as she smiled regretfully.

Jenny felt a surge of indignation at her mother's ingrained conceit and obvious dismissal of Nick as a man worthy of her attention.

"Mother, don't be a snob," Jenny chastised. "After all, I'm a teacher, too."

"Yes, but you don't have to be. You don't have to work at all. You could come to Athens with your father and me and do whatever suits your fancy."

Jenny sighed mightily and smiled impatiently at her mother. "I would go crazy with boredom. I love teaching."

*And I love Nick.* Jenny caught herself before the words could slip out.

Turning toward him with a smile, she held out her hand.

"Let's dance."

As they swirled around the dance floor, she encouraged Nick to ignore her mother.

"She was born snotty. She'll never change, so there isn't a bit of sense in arguing with her."

"She just cares about you."

"I guess. But I'm just not used to it."

He looked at her questioningly and she continued.

"My parents had virtually no time to raise a child. Growing up, I spent most of my time in Nina's care. I became the Butterfly Girl and all they could say was how below us modeling was. Even then, I still wasn't worth much of their time. It wasn't until I was almost killed that they realized they did care for me. They were there for me every minute of every day. For a month. And then they were gone again. They moved to Greece and I haven't seen them but once since then."

"But you still love them. And they love you," Nick insisted.

"You're right," she agreed. "I couldn't pass up this chance to see them."

She didn't say that this might be the last chance she got. She didn't have to. He felt it to the very marrow of his bones and it almost brought him to his knees.

"Jenny, what's the plan here?" he asked solemnly. "There is a plan, right? A plan to keep you safe?"

She shook her head sadly.

"I don't really know, Nick. I left all the details up to Sam."

"And you trust him to keep this lunatic away from you?"

The dance was over and he was leading her off the floor.

"Yes," she lied, "of course."

Nick nodded quickly and scanned the room for anyone suspicious looking. Two men stood out to him. One was the man Daniel Lewiston had been speaking to when they entered. He stood across the room watching Jenny's every move, but making no move

105

toward them. The other was the dark-haired man striding their way, eyes burning with some emotion Nick couldn't name. Nick's arm tightened around her waist protectively.

"You look beautiful, Genevieve," the man said, kissing the hand that Jenny extended to him.

"Sam," she said with an indulgent smile as the man's eyes roamed over her with open approval.

"You haven't changed a bit. You're still as stunning as you ever were."

Jealousy swirled through him as Nick as a blush stole over Jenny's pretty face.

"Thank you."

"After I came to your house the other night, I was afraid it wouldn't work. What miracle worker did you go to?"

As if suddenly remembering him, Jenny whirled to face Nick. She gave him a rather lopsided grimace of apology as she waved toward him.

"Sam Conway, meet Nick Jensen. Nick's sister is the miracle worker responsible for my transformation."

Was she completely oblivious to the animosity that flared between them, Nick wondered, as he shook the man's hand? Could she not know how desperately he needed to know what place Sam Conway held in her life and heart? She had told him there was nothing between them, but everything about the man said something different.

"I think you mean your re-emergence. You were already transformed. You're just re-emerging from the cocoon," Sam said as his eyes scanned the room.

"So, Conway, tell me what the plan is," Nick demanded, looking expectantly at the other man.

"Plan for what?" Sam asked blankly.

"For keeping Jenny safe," Nick growled in frustration. "You do have a plan to keep her safe, don't you?"

Sam straightened his spine and attempted to look unperturbed by Nick's taunt. He was several inches shorter than Nick so he wasn't nearly as intimidating as Jenny suspected he intended to be.

106

"Actually, we have several plans, Coach Jensen." He used the term derogatively, and Jenny wondered how Sam had even known that Nick was a coach. She had never spoken to him about Nick, even though he was obviously trying to make Nick think she had.

"Okay, so what are they?" Nick seemed totally unperturbed by Sam's disdain.

"Our plans depend on what the killer does when he sees her. He may choose to ignore Genevieve's emergence until the end of his own two-week deadline. He may not. We have no idea how his mind works. Will he abduct her again? Kill her the same way he's killed all the other women? The way he nearly killed her six years ago? Or will he simply come into her house and kill her? Until he acts or gives us some hint of his plans, we don't really know which plan to implement to save her."

"So what are you saying? You'll do nothing until after he takes her? Or kills her? The plan is to just sit by and wait until she's suffocating in a plastic bag with a butterfly pinned to her chest?"

Their words cut her like a knife, bringing terror bubbling to the surface as she swayed beneath a fresh onslaught of horror. Without a sound, Nick's arm came around her and he led her to a nearby chair.

"I'm so sorry, Sweetheart" Nick whispered as he squatted before her. He ran his hand over her hair as he studied her pale face in concern. "Just breathe."

He was an idiot, letting Sam get to him like that. He'd been so caught up in sparring with Sam, he wasn't even aware of what their words were doing to her until she'd nearly crumpled in his arms.

To his relief, the color was beginning to return to her cheeks by the time Sam re-appeared with a glass of water, which she took with shaking hands and a soft thank you.

Her eyes met his as she sipped the water, and he longed to erase the shadowed fear he saw there.

"You're going to be fine," he promised, but she only smiled a soft sad smile of acceptance that nearly killed him.

"Genevieve, is that really you?"

"Suzy?" Jenny's face lit up as the pretty blonde bent to hug her tightly.

"It's been ages. I was so excited when I received your mother's invitation. I couldn't pass up the chance to see you." Suzy grasped Jenny's hands. "How are you? Are you still modeling?"

"No. I'm teaching. I haven't modeled since I quit Butterfly."

"Oh, Gen, I'm so glad you used your degree after everything that happened."

"What about you? What have you been up to?"

"Oh, I turned into my mother. I married Richard and I volunteer as a fundraiser for a national charity."

"Richard, really?"

"Yes, he's here somewhere. "Her pretty green eyes scanned the room, before she motioned to the man Nick had noticed watching Jenny earlier. He knocked back a glass of whiskey as they watched. "There he is. Scowling as usual. He hates parties."

"He always did. That was one thing we had in common."

"Yes, well, he hasn't changed much since then." She patted her smooth French braid with perfectly manicured fingers as her eyes roamed over Nick, then Sam. "How about you? Did you ever marry?"

"No, I never did."

Suzy was silent, obviously waiting for her to explain their presence at her side, and Jenny turned toward them.

"Suzy, this is Nick Jensen. Nick this is Suzy Wiggins, my roommate at the Winfield School for Young Ladies."

For the first time, it hit him how different her life had been from his. Boarding school, world traveling parents, ritzy birthday parties in a grand ballroom, and a face that everyone in America recognized. Is that why he'd been so upset when he saw her transformation, because he knew he would never fit into the world where she really belonged?

"You might remember Sam Conway," she was telling Suzy.

"Oh, yes, I think we met at the hospital," Susan smiled and held out her hand.

Sam shook her head indifferently, his eyes scanning the room once more as Jenny turned her attention back to Nick.

"Suzy is the reason I went to work for Butterfly Cosmetics," she told him. "We were sixteen and came from London to Miami with Suzy's mom. Suzy found out Butterfly was having try-outs for their before and after shots. Do you remember those? They took girls, slapped some makeup on them and did before and after pictures."

"I remember. Trish was pretty amazed by some of them."

"A lot of them didn't look all that different," Suzy gushed. "But Jenny was amazing. Before Butterfly, she was a bookworm. She wore these huge, thick glasses and her hair was always a horrible mess. You can't imagine how different she looks when she's not fixed up."

Nick's eyes met Jenny's and he grinned.

"I don't think I'd have too much of a problem with that," he said with a chuckle.

She shrugged off his comment and continued with her recap.

"Anyway, I guess everyone who saw the before and after pictures were as amazed as I was when I saw her, because she became the one and only model for them. They redid their whole ad campaign just for her. My husband says she made them millions." She turned to Jenny. "After you left, I don't think the company was ever the same. Richard didn't work there long, but it seemed Cannon just lost interest in it. I don't know that they ever made another ad. Do you?"

"Not that I know of," Jenny said. "Do you ever see Cannon?"

"No, of course not. He never did like me the way he liked you. His obsession with you was over the top. Richard says it was because you reminded him of his wife."

"His wife?"

"Yes. Apparently, he was married just out of high school, but she died a few years later." She shook her head. "I guess after that, he became a player."

"I guess."

"Oh, here comes Richard now," Susan said with a smile when she looked up and caught a glimpse of her blond, blue-eyed husband coming toward them. Waving, she called out to him. "Richard, I'm over here."

"I wondered where you'd gotten off to," Richard Taylor said as he reached them. "I see you've found her at last."

His eyes scanned Jenny with barely concealed contempt mixed with what Nick suspected was a touch of lust.

Jenny squirmed beneath his glare, and Nick placed a reassuring hand on her shoulder. He met the man's eyes, as he extended his other hand in greeting.

"Nick Jensen," he said gruffly.

"Richard Taylor." He offered a grim smile as he shook Nick's hand. "I worked for Butterfly when Genevieve Lewiston was the girl."

"Richard was the gofer," Susan teased, smiling up at her husband.

"Yeah, Suze, I was the gofer. Let's not forget that." His eyes narrowed as he stared down at his wife before turning to include Jenny in his gaze. "Still am actually. I just work for Suzy's daddy now."

"Richard, don't," Susan pleaded quietly.

"And just in case you don't remember," Richard looked sullenly toward Sam. "I was the number one suspect way back when. But I had an alibi, didn't I, Suzy?"

"You weren't a suspect, Richard. They questioned all the guys," she said, pushing herself to her feet. "It was really nice to see you, Genevieve, but I think we better head home."

"Home?" Richard repeated churlishly. "You mean you don't want to stay and catch up on old times with your friends here? You don't want to make sure they all know I'm infertile as well as incompetent?"

Suzy's father appeared from the other side of the room, and between the two of them, they managed to talk Richard out the door.

"Nice guy," Nick mocked.

"Yeah, I always did love that one." Sam's voice was thick with sarcasm.

"Was he a suspect?" Jenny asked softly and both men turned toward her in unison.

"Everyone was a suspect, Jen," Sam said. "Like your friend said, we looked closely at all the people with Butterfly Cosmetics then."

"I never thought it could be one of them."

"Well, we couldn't be too careful. Now, of course, it seems much more far reaching than that. I don't believe Butterfly Cosmetics had anything at all to do with it. You were the target, and although your position as the Butterfly Girl could have made you more attractive to him, it wasn't the only reason he chose you."

They were interrupted by Helena Lewiston.

"Genevieve, darling, come meet Mr. Costas and his family."

"Excuse me," Jenny said, leaving Nick and Sam behind as she followed her mother away.

"How does he choose them?" Nick asked, letting his eyes roam over the room of partygoers. Could the killer be watching her even now?

"The only thing we've found is that the victims' first names have all been contained in the scientific names of the butterfly specimens he left with the bodies. There's been a Stella, an Anna, a Claudia, and the list goes on. Genevieve's butterfly was the tropical buckeye, *junonia genoveva.* Of course, at the time we found her, were connected the butterfly to her job. We never considered any other possibility. *"*

"And he's been killing since then?"

"Yeah. We have nine women, and God knows how many haven't been found."

"So, what now?"

"Now, we wait," he stated without hesitation.

Nick cursed under his breath and stalked toward Jenny and her mother. He ignored Helena Lewiston's disapproving glare as he took her daughter by the arm and led her to the dance floor.

He pulled her into his arms, breathing in the smooth, sexy smell of her perfume. He held her tightly, loving the way her body fit to his, the way her soft hair tickled his cheek as she leaned her head close to his. He refused to even contemplate the idea of losing her. And he'd be damned if he stood around waiting for some lunatic to come for her. If Sam and his colleagues had no intention of protecting her, he'd do it himself. Fear overwhelmed him and he wanted to sweep her up in his arms and run as fast and as far as he could. But would it help keep her safe? Or would they be followed, hounded to the ends of the earth so an obsessed psycho could catch the only girl who made it out alive?

Nick vowed he would be there for her. He would force her to let him protect her if he had to, but even then, even if he camped out in her yard or on her couch, there would be a moment when he turned his back, a moment when he closed his eyes to sleep. What if that was the moment the killer came? What if that was the very moment he lost her?

"I don't know if I can do this, Jen," he whispered brokenly against her hair.

Jenny nodded against his shoulder, but didn't lift her face. Although she understood how he felt, she couldn't hide the pain his admission caused her.

If she looked at him, she feared she would lose her grip on the tiny bit of control she still had on her ravaged emotions. Her mother would be mortified if she ruined the party with hysterics, and right this moment, hysteria was only one sob away.

They remained silent, swaying to the music of first one song and then another. In his arms, she was as close to heaven as she'd ever been, even with the flames of hell licking at her feet. There was nothing more for them to say. Either he would stay with her until the end or he would walk away. Although she hated the thought of losing him, she hated the idea of the fire consuming him along with her even worse.

She wasn't sure how many songs they danced through before they finally stopped and looked in each other's eyes. She wondered if his deep brown eyes reflected her emotions or if the heartache she saw there was his alone.

# CHAPTER TWENTY-TWO

She scanned the room as they walked off the dance floor, and her heart sank when she saw Sam standing at the door. She knew what his worried gaze meant, and although it terrified her, she knew what needed to be done. There was no reason for her to be here, looking like this, if no one would notice.

She stopped and turned toward Nick, intending to warn him that tomorrow his picture was likely to be in the newspaper, but the words died on her lips. She couldn't bear his anger right here, right now. It would be better to face it when they reached the car, out of sight of everyone but the two of them.

"Let's go home, Nick," she said instead.

"Are you okay? You're looking a little pale."

"I'm fine. Just tired. I haven't been sleeping well." She led him to her parents where her parents were saying good-bye to their guests.

Jenny held her spine straight, willing herself not to cry as she approached them, but feeling her grip slipping with each step.

"Good night, Mama. Good night, Daddy," she said, tears filling her eyes. Her mother's eyes widened as Jenny's voice broke. "I love you."

"What's wrong, darling?" Helena asked in dismay at the uncharacteristic display of emotion.

"Nothing," she tried, trying to smile. "I'm just going to miss you."

"Why don't you come visit us, Princess?" her father asked. "Take a break from work and come to Athens with us."

For a moment, she was tempted to agree. If she got on a plane tonight and flew to Greece, would he follow her there? Or would she be safe? Agreement was there on the tip of her tongue, until she

113

thought of the girls who had already died and the ones who would die if she didn't fulfill the killer's demands.

"I'd love that, Daddy, but I can't," she smiled through her tears. "Maybe I'll see you soon, though."

She kissed them both and with one last good-bye, she turned her back on them for what was possibly the final time.

"Maybe you should go with your parents, Jen," he urged as they were leaving. "That would be the perfect solution."

"You know I can't do that, Nick," she said quietly. "No matter how tempting it might be."

They reached the doors, and Nick pushed them open ahead of her. This is it, she thought as she took a deep breath and stepped out into the cool night air.

Cameras flashed and several reporters scrambled up the steps toward her. Nick moved in front of her, using his broad shoulders to protect her from the view of the cameras. She stood petrified for a moment, blinded by the bright lights and fear.

She wished with all her might that she could fade back into obscurity and return to the life she had made for herself, a life she wanted desperately to include Nick. But they had reached the point of no return.

"It's all right, Nick," she said, laying a trembling hand on his shoulder. "It has to be done."

Nick's blood turned to ice as he turned to look at her. Over her shoulder, his eyes met Sam's triumphant glare and he knew without a doubt that the two of them had planned for this to happen.

With an angry oath, he pushed past the reporters and stalked to where the valet sat in Jenny's car. Let her stand there like a decoy. Let her tell the whole world, including the psycho who wanted to kill her, that she was alive and well. Let her announce to them all that she was the freaking Butterfly Girl. He didn't care. He wouldn't let himself care anymore. For some reason that went far beyond anything he could understand, she had chosen him to lead her like a lamb to the slaughter and he didn't know if he could ever forgive her for that.

114

Silence hung heavy between them as Nick peeled away from the curb, barely giving Sam time to step back from the passenger side of the car. She wanted to beg his forgiveness, but her betrayal was like a living, breathing thing in the car, and she had a feeling mere words would do nothing to dispel it.

"What was that?" he finally growled into the darkness, startling her.

"I'm sorry, Nick." Her voice was quiet, defensive.

With a curse, he turned toward her.

"How could you do that, Jenny? Do you want to die? Do you want him to find you?" he demanded, fear filling his voice.

"He had already found me," she whispered and then grabbed for the dash as he jerked the car to the side of the road and slammed on the brakes.

"What?" Fury ripped through the air between them.

"He knows who I am. He always had. He just wanted me back like I used to be."

"How can you know that?"

Jenny took a ragged breath, willing her tears away, willing him to understand.

"Remember when I told you he sent them a note saying he was coming for me?"

"Yes."

"It said a lot more than that. It said he would kill a girl a week until they produced me."

"You didn't think I'd care to know that?" he asked in an injured tone.

"Nick, I don't think you understand!" she exclaimed. "There is nothing you or I can do about this. It's beyond our control. I cannot refuse to do this! I could never live with myself if I stood by and let other women die, just so I could stay alive!"

He laid his hand on hers.

"I know that, Jenny. I honestly do. From the moment, I met you, I knew you were special, caring, loving, a woman I wanted to get to know. The more I got to know you, the more I realized I could easily fall in love with you." He raked his hand through his hair. "Or maybe I started falling the first time I met you. I don't

115

know. All I know is that I fell for you. Hard. And I thought you felt the same about me."

"I do."

He ignored her quiet confession.

"Now suddenly, you're this woman with a past. A woman who was, and still is, the target of a killer. But I was sure you were safe in our little neighborhood, with me and your friends around to watch over you. You were always beautiful to me, but you were normal, someone we could hide and protect for as long as necessary to keep you safe." He shook his head in bewilderment. "Now, here you are, not just any normal woman, but a woman a whole generation still recognizes. I told myself you could still escape his attention, and if we could make it home tonight, you would go back into hiding until the danger passed. I made it through the night, knowing you were being used as bait for a killer, but hoping there was another way to lure him out into the open."

He took a deep breath, and even in the moonlight, she could see how shadowed his eyes were.

"But there was never another way, was there? When I asked what the plan was, you and Conway both already knew. You knew he was calling the press. You knew they were going to be ready and waiting to capture the return of the Butterfly Girl on film. And you kept that knowledge from me. You chose to let me stand by your side when you walked into the open. Damn it, Jenny, you chose to make me an accomplice to your murder."

"No, Nick."

"Don't lie to me, Jen. We both know it's the truth and we're past the point of saving my feelings. I'm still assimilating all the information I've been bombarded with tonight, and I guess I'm still trying to decide what I'm going to do with it when it finishes processing. When I do, I'll let you know. Until then, I think it would be best if you went about the business of being murdered without my assistance."

There was nothing left for her to say as he put the car in drive and drove her home.

He followed her to her porch, waiting as she unlocked the door with trembling hands. As she pushed open and he made to turn away, but stopped in his tracks. No matter how hurt and angry he was, he couldn't leave her to enter the dark empty house alone. Even when Milt padded to the door, his silence an obvious sign nothing was amiss, Nick couldn't walk away without making certain.

She trailed behind him as he made a thorough sweep of the house, flipping on lights in his wake and leaving no nook or cranny unchecked. He turned to her when they reached the front door, and their eyes held for a long moment.

"Thank you," she said gratefully.

He cupped her cheek in his hand, his thumb stroking her smooth skin. He placed a quick kiss on her forehead and disappeared through the door.

"Nick!" she cried as he neared his truck.

He stopped and turned toward her.

"I don't want to die." She spoke the words so quietly he almost wasn't sure he heard her correctly.

Standing pale and wide-eyed in the yellow glow of the porch light, she reminded him suddenly of a butterfly he had watched it from his seat in a roadside café. He'd watched as it darted in and out of traffic, blown this way and that by the wind from the passing cars. Its ethereal beauty belied the tenacity that kept it fighting for a place to land, until at last the traffic lessened and it settled on yellow line running down the middle of the lanes. It peaceful rest had lasted only a moment before a passing car caught it up in a windstorm and hurled it into the grill of an oncoming car. In the blink of an eye, its valiant struggle was over and it was gone.

He reached her in two bounds, kissing her passionately as she pressed her body close to his and kissed him back with equal fervor. He could taste the salt of her tears as they ran down her face and across their lips.

"You're not going to die. I won't let you," he promised against her lips.

"I don't want to die alone."

117

"You're not alone, Jenny. You'll never be alone again." He swept her up and carried her inside to the sofa. "Don't make me leave."

"You can't stay here, Nick. As a man, you'd be a hero to all the boys in school. Not a good role model, but a hero all the same. As a woman, I'd be a terrible role model and even though there isn't a woman on earth who could blame me for sleeping with you, the standards are much stricter on a woman."

His dark eyes stared into hers, searching for something before he gave a short bark of laughter.

"I'm not leaving you here by yourself, Jen. You'd best grow a thick skin and get used to me being here."

"Sam said he's spoken to the police here. He's trying to arrange some sort or protection so that I'll be under surveillance until the guy's caught."

"I don't care what Sam said. He's a cop in Brevard County, right? That means he has no absolutely no authority to arrange for anything here."

"He's trying,"

"Fine, he's trying. But until he succeeds, I'm not leaving you alone."

# CHAPTER TWENTY-THREE

Ellie scooped the newspaper from the drive, her eyes darting to the truck parked next door.

*Chalk another one up to Ellie Carson, matchmaker extraordinaire*, she thought with a grin.

"What's that satisfied smile for?" Ed asked suspiciously as he came out of the house with an armload of camping gear. His eyes followed hers. "Aha! Way to go, Coach Jensen."

"You don't know he stayed the night," Ellie argued.

"It's barely daylight, and they weren't home yet when we went to bed at midnight. He stayed the night."

"Maybe he was too tired to drive."

"He lives three blocks away."

"Give it up, El, you know what it means the same as I do." He kissed her on the cheek. "It means you're the world's greatest matchmaker."

She laughed as the boys came through the door carrying fishing poles and sleeping bags.

"What's so funny?

Derek looked toward the house, and smiled. "About dang time."

A few more trips in and out of the house, and the guys piled into Ed's old truck, waving good-bye as they pulled away.

Ellie sighed contentedly as they disappeared. The annual fishing trip had begun, which meant her peace and quiet had begun. Until Thursday, her life was her own. There would be no one to haul out of bed in the morning, no breakfast to cook, no lunches to pack. In the afternoon, she could be gone until dark without worrying about supper or she could sit around and read all day long. Whatever she wanted to do, she could do. She would enjoy every minute of it. For about a day. Then she would be ready for them all to come home. She shook her head. She looked forward to their trip all year long, but the minute they were gone, she wondered why she had wanted to be left alone.

Today, she decided, she would go to the library and check out a good thick book that would keep her engrossed for the next few days. On her way home, she'd stop at the nursery and buy some flowers. Her flowerbed needed replenishing and now would be the perfect time to do it. Plus, it would be nice for the boys and Ed to pull in the driveway and see her flowers blooming. With the fishing trip and the flowers, they would know spring had definitely sprung.

Of course, none of that was what she really wanted to do. What she really wanted to do, was to hear exactly how and why Nick ended up staying the night with Jenny. She wouldn't do it now, but when she got home, Jenny better be ready to confess.

Nick woke to Milton's head on his chest. Weak sunlight fought its way through the crack in the curtains as he met the dog's accusing eyes.

"Really, dude?" he moaned, sitting up and trying to massage the kink out of his neck. The futon in Jenny' spare room was anything but comfortable and he felt like he'd slept on a wooden pallet. "I didn't do anything but sleep here."

As if reassured by Nick's words, the dog sauntered out of the room just as Jenny came to the door.

"Nick, I –" she stopped in the doorway, her eyes widening at the sight of him sitting on the edge of the futon dressed in nothing but boxers.

A slow smile spread across his face as her gaze drifted from his head to his thighs before snapping back to his face.

"I hate sleeping in clothes," he explained.

"I, um, I," she looked away, her brow wrinkled. "I made coffee."

She was gone then, hurrying back toward the kitchen as pulled his pants and undershirt on. He refused to put on his dress shirt or the jacket he'd worn last night.

She was sitting at the kitchen table, sipping coffee and nibbling on a bagel slathered with cream cheese. She was dressed in a pair of shorts and a t-shirt, nothing like the long skirts and flowing shirts she'd worn since he'd known her. A light coat of make up made her face soft and pretty, natural. *Like a butterfly.* He could almost hear the commercial from years ago. The though of Jenny, wrapped in a plastic cocoon, a butterfly pinned to her chest shook him and he sat hard in the chair across from her.

"I have to go home and get some clothes," he said, trying to cover up his fear as she looked at him closely. "I can't wear a suit every day."

"You don't need clothes," she said. "I talked to Sam this morning. He checked in across the street yesterday afternoon. He'll be here until they catch the guy."

Jealousy snaked through him at the thought of the man seeing her looking so pretty, of him being right across the street, close enough to wander over to visit, close enough to play the hero if Jenny needed him. Was he really so shallow he'd begrudge her help out of jealousy?

"I'm not leaving you here alone."

"Nick, really. You can't stay. I know Ellie's boys saw your truck here before daylight this morning, but I'd prefer the whole school not see it." She stood up, her hands working nervously at the hem of her shirt, then shorts. "I feel so weird in these clothes."

"You look amazing."

"Thanks, but that doesn't help. I still feel completely out of sorts."

He stood up and walked toward her, catching her face in his hands as soon as he was close enough.

"Let me give you something else to think about," he said before his mouth closed over hers.

Jenny tried to keep her resolve, to make him see she meant business, but she failed miserably. With a sigh, she stepped closer to him, buried her fingers in his hair and kissed him back with equal fervor. Jolts of desire shot between them and he cupped her hips, pushing her against him as the kiss deepened and their control weakened.

She knew she had to stop it. She couldn't let him stay. Sam insisted it was too dangerous for both of them for Nick to be here. The police couldn't keep them both safe and she needed to have full attention to give to watching her back until they caught the killer.

His mouth moved down her neck, and she shivered with pleasure.

"Jen," he murmured, his breath hot and warm against her skin. "I want you."

It took every bit of strength she had to say, "You've got to go home, Nick."

He went completely still. She held her breath, waiting for his refusal, frightened by the utter silence between them. Finally, he pushed away, staring at her with bleak injured eyes. Her heart ached from causing him pain, and she reached out a hand.

"Nick, I'm sorry." The last word faded away as he turned and stalked from the room.

Knowing she had to let him leave, she stayed where she was, cringing as the slamming of the front door was followed by the sound of his truck backing out of her drive. Then and only then did she give in to her tears of frustration.

After a few moments of self-pity, she sniffed back her tears and pushed herself away from the counter. Enough was enough. There was no guarantee she wasn't going to die, but there was no guarantee she was either. But she wasn't dead this moment, so she still had time, and she intended to use it wisely.

She picked up the telephone and dialed her parents' number.

"Hello?" Her dad sounded half asleep.

"Hi, Dad. I just wanted to tell you and Mom how wonderful everything was last night. Do you think we could get together before you leave?"

"We'd love to see you again, but we're leaving tomorrow and we have meetings for the rest of the day today and into tonight. We need to get an early start tomorrow so we can catch our flight." He paused to listen to her mother. "You mother wants you to visit us in the fall. I'll arrange to have a few days free during your stay. You and your mother can shop and do whatever it is you like to do. We'll make the arrangements. Can you do that, Genevieve?"

"I'll try, Daddy." They grew silent and finally, she added. "I love you both, tell Mama. Good-bye."

She hung up and dialed Ellie's number. Before it could ring, there was knock on her back door and Ellie let herself in.

"Jenny?" she screeched in surprise. "My God, you're gorgeous!"

"Thanks," Jenny smiled. "Are you surprised?"

"For sure," Ellie laughed.

"Ed and the boys are gone, I take it?"

"Yes, they left before daylight. I've been to the library and the garden shop." She smiled knowingly. "So, spill, sister. What was Nick's truck still doing here this morning? Or do I even need to ask?"

"It isn't what you think," Jenny objected. "He stayed because I couldn't convince him I'd be safe if he left. He slept on the futon in the spare room."

"The futon? Are you crazy?"

"Maybe, but I couldn't sleep with him, El. Not now. Maybe not ever, but definitely not until the murderer is caught."

"So was Nick furious when he realized who you were?"

"I think he was more hurt I hadn't told him, but he got over it pretty quickly. I don't know if he's completely over the fact that Sam called the press."

Ellie's look of horror told Jenny she understood the repercussions.

"So now what?"

"Now, we go ahead with our annual girls' night."

It had become an annual tradition for them to get together for one night of pizza, wine and girl talk while Ed and the boys were away. Jenny saw no reason not to do it this year. In fact, she saw every reason to do it.

"Are you sure?"

"Positive, but I have one rule. No talking about murders, past, present or potential."

"Agreed," Ellie hugged her tightly. "I'll see you at my house about six thirty or seven."

123

"Wait until the boys see you," Ellie said as they sat in her house hours later. "I'll have to lock them up. Darn it, Jenny, I may have to lock Ed up. I would never have let him move you in next door if I had known you looked like this! Heck, I wouldn't even have let him show you houses alone."

Jenny chuckled and rolled her eyes. "Ed's crazy about you and you know it. He wouldn't have noticed what I looked like either way."

"He is pretty great isn't he?"

"He's a real gem."

"Speaking of real gems, what's going on with yours?"

Jenny leaned back and closed her eyes, letting the relaxing effects of the wine seep through her.

"I think I'm in love," she said quietly.

"Really? With Nick?" Ellie squealed, sitting up quickly.

"Really, and of course with Nick. Who else?"

"Your cop, what's his name? Sam?" Ellie cocked her head to one side.

"What about him?"

"Didn't you and he have a relationship once?"

"How in the world would you know that?" She wasn't sure if she was more surprised or embarrassed.

"For heaven's sake, Jenny, I've made a life out of trying to match you up with the right man. You don't think I'd notice when you suddenly have two men who can't keep their eyes off of you?"

"You've never seen Sam and me together," Jenny laughed.

"But I've seen him cruising through the neighborhood, keeping an eye on things." Ellie held her hand up for Jenny to keep quiet. "I know it's kind of his job, but he's not even a cop in St. Johns County. So renting a room across the street from your house seems a little over the top."

"Sam's a little overzealous about his job."

"I don't think his job is his only obsession, Jen." She shrugged. "But I guess it's not the worst thing in the world to have two gorgeous men obsessed with you."

# CHAPTER TWENTY-FOUR

May 1, 2006
Miami Beach
*Pyrisitia lisa,* Little Yellow

*Finding Lisa Martin was like finding the golden egg. A tiny woman with golden blonde hair that glistened in the sunlight filtering through the windows of the hotel, she was as perfect as they came. The tiny yellow butterfly in the box at home came to mind, but he knew her name couldn't possibly be Lisa.*

*He was rounding the corner near his room when he heard a voice calling out to her. He turned, sure his mind was playing tricks on him, but her friend called her name again as she came bouncing down the hallway to meet her.*

*He knew then that she was meant to be one of his butterflies. He could hardly wait to take her. She was so tiny, so fragile looking. So like the picture in Vanessa's book.*

*Only one thing bothered him about her; she wasn't vulnerable. She was young, full of life, and obviously in love with the tall blond boy who lay beside her on the beach that afternoon. She would never come to him willingly. He closed his eyes regretting the knowledge that he would have to force her.*

*He had never forced any of his butterflies before, but she was too perfect to pass up. He would have to think of a way to get her away from the group of friends she was traveling with so that it was easier to convince her to come with him, or to simply overpower her if need be.*

*Fate was with him as he entered the hotel lounge that night. Lisa sat at the bar, obviously trying to drink herself into oblivion. It wasn't hard to coax her into telling him what the problem was. Her boyfriend had been flirting with her best friend all day, and she'd had enough of it. She had left them both at a club down the road.*

*With a sympathetic smile, he bought her a drink.*

*They talked for a while before she got down from her barstool, swaying precariously.*

*"Let me help you to your room," he murmured, loud enough for the bartender to hear him.*

*There was nothing about the description the bartender would give that would lead the police to him. His disguises were always impeccable.*

*By the time they passed the door to the beach, she was nearly unconscious and he knew it was time. He pushed open the door, and after a few steps away from the hotel, swung her up in his arms and carried her to his waiting car.*

*When it was done and Lisa slept in her airtight chrysalis on the side of A1A, he went home and pinned the tiny yellow butterfly in its place beside the others.*

# CHAPTER TWENTY-FIVE

Ellie was sitting on the porch swing listening to the rain and enjoying the cooling breeze it brought with it when a police car pulled to a stop on the narrow street in front of her house. Had something happened to Ed or the boys? Oh, God, what would she do if they were hurt or, worse yet, dead?

"Can I help you?" she said, her voice hoarse with fear.

The taller of the two spoke. "Ma'am, I'm Officer Kelly and this is Officer Bowen. We're looking for Genevieve Lewiston."

"Genevieve?" she repeated blankly.

Then, as the shock of seeing them striding purposefully toward her dissipated, the name clicked. They were looking for Jenny. The boys were fine. Ed was fine. She breathed a sigh of relief and glanced at the house next door.

"Do you know her?" Officer Kelly asked.

"Yes, of course, she lives next door."

"Thank you, ma'am." Officer Bowen, tipped his hat at her as he followed his partner across her drive and up to Jenny's door.

"I don't think she's home," Ellie said, getting control of herself and following behind them. "She left this morning and I haven't seen her since. If you'd like to come in, I'll call her and see when she should be here."

Once she and the officers were in the house, Ellie dialed Jenny's cell phone. She left a quick message when the voice mail picked up.

She tried Nick, who she was certain was in the middle of ball practice, and then tried Nina's store. Nina answered on the first ring, but she hadn't seen Jenny either.

When it was obvious she wasn't going to locate Jenny so easily, Officer Kelly handed her his card.

127

"Have your friend call this number as soon as you talk to her. It's extremely important that we speak to her." His stern gaze met Ellie's.

"Is this about what happened to her before?" she asked. "She knows about the other murders. Sam, I'm sorry I'm not sure of his last name, but he's a detective. He told her."

"A detective you say? So she's been contacted already?"

"Yes, he's the detective who helped her after she was kidnapped."

"And he's told her what's happening now?"

"Yes. He's staying at the inn just across the street." She motioned to the inn and the policemen followed her gaze.

"Thank you for your help, ma'am. I'd still like to speak with Ms. Lewiston when she's available. If you'll tell her we stopped by, I'd appreciate it."

"Oh, of course," Ellie said. She followed them back outside, watching as they crossed the street to the inn.

Where was Jenny? She had been worried about Jenny before but somehow their presence made it more real and urgent. She hurried back into the house and called Jenny's number again and again and received no answer. Through the window, she saw the police car pull away. Should she call them back and tell them she was worried about Jenny? Should she be worried? Could the killer have acted that fast? Could he already have her?

Jenny strolled along the beach while Milton bounded ahead of her, dodging in and out of the waves after seagulls and sandpipers. The birds quickly flew away and he looked toward the sky before searching the stretch of sand for the spot where they had landed.

There were few people here today. It was still a little early for the summer tourist season, and the day had turned cloudy as an approaching front pushed colder, wetter weather south into Florida. Jenny loved to be here on days like this. She loved to watch the waves roll in, gray against the darkening sky. These kinds of days were perfect to come out and saunter down the shoreline, before school was out for the summer and before the really warm weather settled in. It was peaceful and quiet, and the shells were undisturbed by too many feet and tires. This was her favorite place to come and regroup. Today, she was here to find peace.

It had been six years and she understood many people would have needed the closure of having him caught and brought to justice. She simply wanted to go on and forget that it ever happened, being thankful she survived. She loved teaching and didn't really mind her self-imposed plainness. She was happy, and had finally found someone who wanted to be with her.

Picking up a handful of seashells, she tossed them one by one into the ocean. She could still see Nick's face when she'd pushed him away yesterday morning. Why couldn't he understand she had no choice? She couldn't be distracted, couldn't let her guard down or let him get in the way of what needed to be done. Sam had made clear that he needed her full attention on luring the killer to her. When that was done, if she lived to see it, would Nick forgive her? Would they be able to start again? His hurt, angry eyes filled her mind and with a cry, she hurled the rest of the shells into the ocean.

Why had the past come back to haunt her now, when she had finally found the one and only thing she'd been missing?

"Beautiful day for a barbeque, huh?" Trish asked as she dropped to the chair beside Nick. "The gray skies match your mood. Does that have something to do with Jenny not being here?"

"I don't want to talk about it, Trish," he said without taking his eyes from the Tolomato River, which flowed quietly past his parents' backyard on its way to the Atlantic Ocean. "Not that that's ever stopped you."

"Yeah, it's not going to stop me this time either."

"I never thought it would."

"You can't still be mad her about not telling you what she did as a teenager. So there must be something else."

"She lied to me."

She was quiet for so long, he breathed a sigh of relief. Usually she was much more persistent. He moaned in disappointment when she took a deep breath and he realized she was about to say something.

"You're a good man, Nick, but you are a real moron."

129

He shook his head wryly. "You're probably right about that, Sis."

His cell phone rang and he answered it with a curt hello.

"Nick, is Jenny with you? Have you seen her?" Ellie's frantic questions caught him off guard.

"No, I haven't seen her since yesterday. Why?"

"She hasn't been home all day. The police came looking for her, but she's not there, and I can't get her to answer her phone. I'm worried, Nick."

"The police? A guy named Sam?"

"No, no, not Sam. There were two of them. They wanted to talk to her. She wasn't home. They went over to the inn to talk to Sam."

"Did they talk to him?" He was up, crossing the yard with long strides as Trish called after him.

"I guess so. I saw them leaving a little while later."

The racing of his heart slowed a little as he realized the cops from both counties were working together to keep her safe.

"I'm sure she's fine, Ellie," he assured her.

"Why aren't you with her?"

A normal line of questioning had to mean Ellie had reached the same conclusion he had.

"Didn't she tell you?"

"She told me, yes, but it didn't make a bit of sense to me."

"Me either."

"But you're just going to let her base your relationship on that kind of bull?"

He sighed.

"Let me know when you see her, El."

"You'll come when I call?"

"I'll be there in next to no time."

"Good. I'll talk to you then."

# CHAPTER TWENTY-SIX

Jenny grabbed the ringing phone as she dashed through the rain on her way to her front door.

"Jenny?" Ed Carson's voice was deep with worry. "Have you seen Ellie?"

"I'm just getting in, Ed. Is something wrong?" She pushed open the door and Milt joined her on the porch.

"No, no, it's just that I always call her the second afternoon we're up here. She usually picks up on the first or second ring because she's expecting the call. I've been calling her since five and haven't gotten an answer."

"The van is in the drive and the kitchen light is on. She must be there."

Milt barked once before bounding off the porch and running toward Ellie's house.

"I can hear the rain coming down, Jen. Maybe the service is out."

"Did you try her cell?"

"I did, but it goes straight to voice mail. I figure she forgot to charge it."

"That sounds about right. Do you want me to run over and let her use my phone?"

"Not now. Wait until it quits raining. If I haven't gotten hold of her in a few hours, I'll call you back."

"Okay. I'll run over as soon as the rain stops."

She hung up the phone, realizing Milt was pawing at the gate to the Carsons' backyard.

"Milt!" she called. "Come out of the rain. I don't want to have to give you another bath."

Milt's whining grew louder as she continued to yell for him.

She threw her purse in the house, and stalked across the yard toward him.

"You are in big trouble buster," she warned, but stopped cold when Milt began to dig frantically beneath the gate as if desperate to get to the other side. Something was wrong.

Her shaking hand pushed the latch, letting the gate swing open so that in the bright flash of lightning that followed, she could clearly see the plastic-shrouded bundle beneath the huge live oak.

"Oh, God," she breathed as she sank to her knees, unable to go any further. Her hands fumbled for her cell phone and she dialed 911, screaming for help as she waited.

She could hear shouting voices and pounding feet running in her direction, but she remained where she was, praying for the nightmare to end.

"Genevieve," Sam's voice was close to her hear as his hands came around her, lifting her to her feet. "You need to move."

She realized then, that the paramedics were there.

She clung to him, letting him lead her to the porch. Her cell phone rang and she answered it with a breathless cry.

"Jenny?" Ed's terror shot through the phone line straight into Jenny's heart. Jenny took a breath that was more a ragged sob.

"You and the boys need to come home, Ed."

"What's going on, Dad?" she heard Derek ask in the background. Then, in a panicked voice, "Dad! Dad! Uncle Ken!"

She waited for Ed's brother to come on the line and told him there had been an accident and he needed to get Ed and the boys home immediately. Without thought, she stood up and walked to the fence, watching as the paramedics tried to resuscitate her best friend.

They put Ellie on the gurney and although Sam reached out to stop her, Jenny pushed past him to follow them to the waiting ambulance. She didn't wait for them to ask before climbing inside, holding Ellie's hand as she prayed for her life.

Terror flooded him when Nick saw the ambulance pull away from Jenny's street. He sped down her street, slamming to a stop in

132

front of the Carson house where two police cars were pulled into the drive.

He jumped out of his car, her name roaring from his lips.

"Jenny!" He came through the back gate, his heart freezing in his chest at the sight of the rumpled plastic, the dead butterfly, and the crime scene markers.

"Sorry, sir, you can't come back here," a short stocky police officer said.

"Ok," he nodded blankly.

"Are you okay? Do you know her?"

Do, not did. Was there still hope?

"Yes."

"She's gone in the ambulance."

"She's alive?"

"She was when she left. Barely."

He ran to his car, peeling down the road, heedless of speed limits or safety zones.

He rushed through the emergency room doors, his eyes scanning every face. He cried out when he met her wide, turquoise eyes, terrified but alive, and he stumbled toward her, catching her against him as he kissed her.

"You're alive," he whispered. "Thank God."

She was sobbing against his chest and he finally made out her words, his heart dropping as he realized what she was saying.

"Ellie. He got Ellie."

# CHAPTER TWENTY-SEVEN

Jenny slipped through the gate that led to the Carsons' backyard. Ed stood silently beneath the tree where she found Ellie. His clothes were the same rumpled clothes he'd worn home from his trip and thick stubble covered his chin.

"What will we do without her?" he said as she came toward him.

"She's not going to die."

"It's been three days, Jen. Every day it becomes less likely she'll wake up." He scrubbed a hand over his face. "I can't let the boys see me like this. They're both at the hospital sitting with her. I told them I had to come home to get a shower, shave. I don't like leaving them there by themselves, but truthfully, I just needed a few minutes to break down."

His voice broke and she swallowed the lump in her throat.

"Why don't you do what you told the boys you were going to do? Take a shower. Shave. Rest for a little while. I'll go sit with the boys."

"Would you?" he asked, his eyes and voice showing his exhaustion.

"Of course. It's the least I can do."

"Jenny," he said, turning toward her again, "Ellie really loves you. According to her, moving you in next door was the best present I ever gave her. She would never want you to feel like this was your fault."

"I love her, too, Ed, and I wish to God he would just have taken me instead of her."

Nick was pulling up behind her car when she came out of her house a little while later.

"Come on, I'll drive you over," he ordered, opening the truck door and jumping out. "I can drive, Nick," she protested weakly.

"Get in this truck right now, Jenny."

Without further protest, she climbed obediently in and let him drive her to the hospital. The boys met her at the elevators, hopeful grins on their youthful faces.

"The doctors say Mom might be improving some," Derek said. "She's opened her eyes a time or two this morning."

"Really? Oh, boys, that's wonderful! Can we see her?"

"We just did," Eddie said. "I don't think anyone else can go in for an hour or something like that."

"I'll just wait then." She looked at Nick. "Do you mind?"

"Of course not. You guys want to go down and get a burger while Jen stays up here?"

"I'm not hungry," Eddie protested, but his stomach picked that moment to betray him by rumbling, and Jenny put her hand on his shoulder.

"Go eat, Eddie. I promise your Mom will be fine while you're gone."

He followed his brother and Nick to the elevator, looking back once before the doors closed behind them.

"Are you here with Ellie Carson's family?" a petite, dark-haired nurse asked. When Jenny nodded, she crooked her finger toward the room. "You can visit her for a few minutes if you want. She seems to be responding a little more so it can't hurt to talk to her as if she can hear you."

"Hey, Ellie," she leaned close to her, "you need to wake up. Ed and the boys are frantic. They're home, you know. And they need you to come home, too. Heck, I need you to come home. I have to tell you how crazy I am about Nick."

"How is she?" Sam asked and she spun around to him.

"I didn't think they'd let anyone else in."

"I've been here. They know I'm working on the case."

He moved into the room, his eyes scanning Ellie and the machines.

"They think she's improving some. The nurse said she responded to some pain stimuli this morning. It could mean nothing, but it could mean she's coming out of it. The boys are ecstatic."

136

"I bet they are. It's hard to lose someone you love. Your mother, your wife. Your friend."

There was a sadness in his eyes she had only seen a few times since she met him. Sam had always been quiet about his personal life and she wondered now who he had loved and lost.

He cupped his hand around her upper arm. "Her husband tells me the two of you were the best of friends."

"Yes, we are," she said. "I've never had a friend like Ellie. I can't imagine losing her. We've been friends since the day I moved in next door. Ed sold me my house. Did you know that? He was the first real estate agent I went to and the house next door to them had just been put on the market. It was the third house he showed me, and I fell in love with it as soon as I saw it."

"It suits you well. It's a very pretty house." His eyes met hers. "I thought about you over the years, wondered how you were and what your life was like. I wondered if you were still terrified, waking up with nightmares and startling at every little movement."

She shook her head. "I rarely dream about it anymore. I'm still nervous sometimes, especially in the spring, but for the most part, I'm fine."

"I'm glad you found peace here, Genevieve."

"I just don't understand why he did this. I mean, I did what he asked, but he still tried to kill Ellie. It doesn't make sense."

As if anything about any of it made sense.

"We're working on trying to figure out what we missed. Was there a reason he targeted Ellie Carson other than she was your friend? The butterfly told us nothing except he's willing to deviate from his signature when it fits his needs. Every other woman he's killed shared her name with a butterfly. Ellie Carson didn't." He pulled a small notepad from his pocket and scanned a page. "The butterfly he left was her was a Gulf Fritillary. Her scientific name is *agraulis vanilla*e. No connection that we can see with Ms. Carson, but maybe he's something only he understands. Did he target her because of that? Was it only because she was your friend? Or was there another reason we aren't even seeing?"

"What do you think?"

137

"I think I've got to get going. We have a case meeting at three down at the station."

He stepped closer and pressed his lips to her cheek.

"Thank you, Sam," she said. "I owe you so much."

"You've never owed me a thing, Genevieve." He ran a gentle hand down her hair. "I can't believe how beautiful you look. I could almost believe we turned back the clock."

"I'm not looking to turn back the clock, Sam," she said. "I just want it to keep right on ticking."

"Hello, Ellie."

The voice whispered through the darkness she lived in, making her ache with fear.

"Genevieve came home much sooner than I expected the night I visited you." His footsteps came closer. "I thought for certain you would be dead by the time they found you. Not that it matters. Genevieve was the only one who survived. And she'll keep that distinction."

If she hadn't already been so cold, she would have frozen solid from the chill that rushed through her as he bent closer to her.

"You almost made it, Ellie. But in the end, you succumbed as all the rest of them did. Don't worry, though, Genevieve will join you soon." She felt the sharp prick of the needle. "Your transformation is complete now. You will awake in heaven, a butterfly."

Although her mind screamed out a denial, it was an easy death; just a soft whisper of breath and she was gone.

# CHAPTER TWENTY-EIGHT

May, 2011
Key West
Julia Heliconian, *dryas Julia*

*Julia Dane was dying. He could see her breath becoming more labored, and even in her drug-induced sleep, she tossed a little, searching for air. With something akin to awe, he sat back and watched her transformation.*

*It never ceased to amaze him when he found the perfect girl. It required so much more than just the same name. If it were only that, he would have Vanessa's box filled by now. For them to be perfect there had to be another link that reminded him of the butterflies they would become.*

*Julia had orange hair. Not the gaudy kind women get from a bottle, but the pretty, natural tint that would have earned her the nickname "carrot top" from her crueler playmates.*

*He'd known she was the one as soon as she looked at him with those huge dark eyes so filled with pain and vulnerability. Her hair was pulled back at the nape of her neck with a bow, but little wisps of it curled around her face, and he'd just known she would be the next butterfly to join Vanessa in heaven.*

*The Julia butterfly was one of Vanessa's favorites, always eliciting a joyful cry when it fluttered by, seeking the warmth of the Florida sun on its wings.*

*Was that why Julia Dane came here? Was she, too, seeking the warmth, escaping the chill of disillusionment? Escaping the bone chilling cold of lost love? Isn't that why they were all here in this place, on these islands, to escape the reality of the cold, cruel world and find a safe harbor where the sun always shone, and no one asked questions about the things they sought to forget?*

*Usually, he knew something about their lives before he sent his butterflies to heaven, but Julia was an easy conquest. He picked her up in a bar on Duval Street, and she came back to his hotel with him, no questions asked.*

*When he saw that her chest no longer rose and fell gently within her chrysalis, he rose to his feet. Her futile efforts to breathe had been abandoned, as had the body that once housed her soul, now it was only a matter of setting her free.*

*She would be happy in the spot he picked for her, deep in the campground of Bahia Honda, amidst the mangroves and scrub oaks. One of the many campers there would find her sooner rather than later, but he would be headed North long before that happened.*

# CHAPTER TWENTY-NINE

Jenny barely noticed as the first fat raindrops fell into the newly turned earth of Ellie's grave. Ellie had been buried three days ago, and the investigation into her murder had hit the same brick wall that all of the previous murders had. Although she was found sooner than the rest, the rain had washed away any clue the killer might have left behind. Which meant he was still out there biding his time waiting for God knew what before striking again.

Now, Jenny stood where she was, eyes closed against the memory of Ed and the boys standing there stoically, tears coursing down their cheeks as they received the mourners who had come to bid farewell and offer their condolences. How would they carry on now that Ellie was gone? Derek and Eddie were still children, still very much in need of their mother, yet they would face every day without her. The only comfort to be had was the assurance that Ellie had lived and loved to the fullest extent.

*You can't be dead if you were never alive, Jen.* As clearly as if Ellie was standing right in front of her, her words echoed through Jenny's mind.

Ellie had lived every single day as if it would be her last, and even now that her life was over, Jenny doubted Ellie would have done one single thing differently. She had known who she was, accepted herself and the people around her without reservation. She had loved well, lived well, and died a horrible death that Jenny would never forgive herself for.

She shuddered at the thought of Ellie feeling the mind-numbing panic of the plastic covering her face, her breath growing shallow as her mind fought to remain lucid and her lungs fought for air.

"I'm sorry, Ellie, so sorry." Her voice was drowned out by a crack of thunder, calling her attention to the fact that she was soaking wet and standing out in the open in the middle of a thunderstorm.

She rushed toward Nick's waiting truck, crying out when a bolt of lightning flashed through the sky. She slid across the street, until she was flush with Nick's side, and he held her close as she shivered against him.

"I'm getting you soaked," she said, trying to slide away from him.

"It's fine. Just stay where you are." His arm tightened and he pressed a kiss to the top of her head, murmuring some soothing noise against her head.

The night Ellie died, Nick informed Jenny, and in turn Sam, that he had absolutely no intention of leaving Jenny's side. If the killer got her, it wouldn't be on his watch. So far, he'd made good on that promise. He slept, ate, and did everything else at her house, regardless of her protests. Of course, her protests had been halfhearted at best. She was petrified and heartbroken and she needed him there more than she cared to admit.

Ellie would be thrilled.

Tears clouded her vision as the thought. How many times had Ellie told her Nick was for her? Had she really known Nick was everything Jenny had ever wanted? Had Ellie known how head over heels in love she would fall? Had she known that as soon he touched her, Jenny would want everything life with him had to offer?

As they drove slowly through town, Nick kept a hold on Jenny. He couldn't seem to get enough of having her next to him. He wanted to comfort her, to keep her safe, but he also wanted her. He wanted her the way a man wants a woman. He wanted to hold her, touch her, kiss her at leisure. He wanted to make love to her.

He held back because he knew it wouldn't be fair to her right now. She was too hurt and vulnerable. He predicted he could easily coax her into bed, but when he did, he wanted her to have no regrets. He wanted her to want him, not just the comfort of another human touch, but him alone.

142

He could be patient. As far as he was concerned, they had the rest of their lives.

"Stop!" she cried, startling him out of his thoughts.

"What is it?"

"That man," she said pointing to a tall blond man dashing toward the cigar shop. "I think I know him. It's been so long since I saw him, I'm not sure."

"Who is he?"

"Cannon Brockway." She pressed her face to the window to get a better look. "He owns Butterfly Cosmetics, and he was the last person I talked to the night of my abduction."

She was out of the car, rushing through the rain before he could stop her.

"Damn it, Jen," he muttered as he searched for a parking spot. By the time he found one, she was disappearing through the cigar shop door.

"Cannon?" She touched the man's arm and he turned toward her.

The change in him was so dramatic her breath caught in her throat. The piercing blue eyes were red-rimmed and dull from the alcohol tingeing his breath, and deep crevices lined his ruddy face.

"Genevieve?" he slurred. "Is it really you, girl?"

"Yes. How are you Cannon?" Sadness swept through her. She knew how he was.

"You've grown up. Even prettier now than you were then." He ran a hand down her hair, resting it on her shoulder as he swayed slightly. "I lost it all, you know?"

"I'm so sorry to hear that."

"After you left, it fell apart. Evan and me, we just couldn't seem to work out an ad, couldn't find another girl like you. Couldn't think of anything else. So, I sold it all to some outfit from China." His laughter was a bitter heartbreaking sound. "Made out like a bandit. But never could seem to get it together."

"There you are," Nick said, coming up to them. His eyes took in Cannon's arm on her shoulder and he raised his eyebrows questioningly.

143

"Nick, hi. This is Cannon Brockway. Cannon, this is Nick Jensen."

"Good to meet you," Nick said sticking out a hand, which Cannon grabbed with what looked to be bone-crushing enthusiasm.

"Nick, you lucky dog. I tried to woo her, you know, but she always shot me down." He made a whistling noise as he gestured a nosedive with his thumb. "Shot. Me. Down."

Nick's mouth twitched and his eyes danced with amusement.

"She was the only one who did though. All the other girls were more than willing, but Genevieve was special."

"Are you here visiting?"

"Sure, sure." His eyes darted around the store. "Came to get a cigar and some champagne."

"Are you celebrating something?" Nick asked.

"Marriage." A frown creased his brow. "My marriage."

"Is your wife here with you?"

Tears welled in his eyes, and his lips trembled as he shook his head.

"She hasn't been here in a long, long time, but I still feel her here. I still hear her laughter. Still see her sitting by the ocean, Cohiba in hand." He took a deep breath of the tobacco-scented air. "My girl loved a good cigar."

"Where are you staying, Cannon? Can we give you a ride home?"

He shook his head, a sad smile playing about his mouth.

"No, Genevieve, but thank you. I'm going to walk these streets as if she's here beside me. And when I'm done I'm going home."

He took her hand, bringing it to his lips for a lingering kiss.

"It was good to see you, Sweetheart." He turned to Nick. "You take care of her, dude. Keep her close. She'll disappear in the blink of an eye. Like a butterfly freed from a bell jar, she'll fly away to parts unknown."

He turned away then, dismissing them as if he were still the master of his universe.

"C'mon," Nick took her arm and dragged her toward the door.

"But, Nick," she protested.

"No, buts, Jen," he said. "We're out of here."

144

"I'm worried about him."

"I'm worried about you."

The rain had stopped, but the streets were still nearly empty of people as he pulled her along.

"What the hell were you thinking going after him like that?" he demanded. "He was the last person to see you before you were nearly killed. What if he's the killer?"

She dug in her feet, forcing him to stop. How had that idea never occurred to her? It wasn't possible, she realized. Cannon might have been a player, he might be a drunk now, but he wasn't a killer.

"I'll pick you up and carry you if I have to," he warned.

When she laughed, he did just that, scooping her up over his shoulder and stalking toward the truck. By the time, he tossed her inside, she was laughing for the first time in days. She grasped his face, pulling it toward her own.

"I love you, Nick," she said, as she captured his mouth with hers.

# CHAPTER THIRTY

"You're sure you don't want to come with us?"

"Positive," Officer Franklin Kelly answered, bending to kiss his wife's cheek. "You and the kids go have a good time. Tell everyone I'm sorry I couldn't make it. Neil and I are working on something."

"That old beater in the driveway or the six-pack in the fridge?"

"Neither," he chuckled. "Actually, we've got a witness in Lake City that we think may be able to give us a description of a suspect. The sheriff's office out there is supposed to call us if she does."

"Fine, I'll see you in a few hours." She kissed him good-bye, pulling the door shut just as his cell phone rang.

"We've got the description, Frank," Neil told him. "I'm emailing you the sketch now. I've got a real good feeling about this. We'll nail him before he can get to another girl."

He sat at his desk, pulled up the email and opened the attachment.

"Shit!" he muttered. "Shit!"

*The picture in the paper didn't do her justice. He had seen her the night of her father's birthday party, watched her emerge from the ballroom and his breath had wedged in his chest. She was even prettier than she had been six years ago. Then, she had been young, confident, and innocent. Now, she was aware of her own vulnerability, uncertain of what tomorrow held and frightened by the evil she knew walked the earth. Her eyes scanned the people around her, wondering if each of them was the one who was after her.*

He was glad she would be his last one. She would complete the circle of butterflies that surrounded Vanessa's in the display. When he looked at it, he could imagine them in heaven, surrounding Vanessa with their outstretched wings.

He caressed the wings of each specimen as he recalled the girl who shared its name. Anna Steinberg, the petite, perky newscaster he released on the bank of the Suwannee River.

Stella Dobbins, the tall, slender brunette released in the Everglades. Claudia, the bronze goddess he left in the pasture in Ocala.

Diana, the black-haired belly dancer he met at a themed restaurant in Kissimmee. She had been working there to put her younger sister through school after their parents had gone to prison for drug possession. She was somewhere in an orange grove in Winter Haven.

Sara came the year after Genevieve, and was one of his favorites. With her white-blonde hair and huge blue eyes, she reminded her of the gossamer wings of the butterfly. Her husband ran off after two months of marriage, leaving her broken-hearted and vulnerable. She had been his easiest capture yet.

But, of course, those on the rebound were always easy. He'd left her in a peach orchard just this side of the Florida-Georgia line.

Lisa and Julia followed, both young and beautiful.

Rita had been last year. She was the reason he decided this year would be his last. Women were wiser than they had been just a few years ago. They were warned by the media at every turn not to drink anything someone gave them. Some listened, some didn't. Rita listened. And when he offered her a drink at the party he crashed, she flatly refused. She never drank a drink she looked away from, and she never drank one she didn't get directly from the bartender. He actually had to follow her home and take her by force, leaving a huge bruise on her face, something he had never done before. When she was finally wrapped up in her chrysalis, he pinned the specimen to the board and realized that there was only room for one more.

That's when his mind turned to the one who got away...

148

# CHAPTER THIRTY-ONE

Jenny's stomach was in knots as she sat on a blanket in the park, waiting for Nick's baseball practice to end. Nearby, Milt and one of the neighborhood boys played ball, but she couldn't find her usual enjoyment in watching them. She was too tense and on edge, waiting, wondering when it would happen. How long would she have to wait until the killer finally made his move? It had been a week since Ellie's funeral. A week of watching and waiting, feeling the touch of his eyes on her skin, the prickle of his breath on her neck. He was out there somewhere, and he knew exactly where she was. Officer Franklin Kelly had come to her house last night, leaving a card in her front door asking her to call him as soon as possible.

A shadow fell across her, and she looked up. Shading her eyes, she smiled up at Nick.

"Hi."

"Hi, yourself." he dropped down beside her. He cupped her head in his hand and pulled her face to his for a kiss.

"How was practice?" she asked, looking back toward the boy and dog that were rolling around on the ground, wrestling for the ball.

"Great. You haven't heard from the cops again?"

"Sam said he would take care of it when I showed him the card last night. He hasn't called, so I assume he either hasn't reached them or it wasn't a big deal."

"Ms. Lewis!"

"Speak of the devil," Nick said under his breath.

"That's not Officer Kelly. It's his partner. Bowen, I think."

"Close enough."

Jenny watched in horror as a dark colored car rounded the corner coming from the direction of her house. The horror unfolded so fast Jenny wasn't certain of anything, except that when sped away, it left the young blond officer lying in the middle of the quiet suburban street.

Jenny scrambled to her feet, rushing toward him. She knelt beside his broken body as Nick shouted information at the 911 dispatcher.

The officer looked toward her, his eyes glazed with pain and something she didn't want to see this close.

"You," he whispered brokenly, stopping for a moment as if gathering enough strength to continue, "you know him."

Death wiped the pain from his eyes. Jenny tried to stand, to move away from him, but her legs refused to hold her up. She stumbled back from her place by his side.

"Jenny," Nick said as he caught her elbows and helped her to her feet.

She looked up into Nick's dark, concerned eyes, then back to the man lying dead behind her as his words echoed in her mind.

*You know him.*

"No!" she cried, pushing away from Nick.

He stared at her in surprise as she backed away from him. Her eyes darted from person to person as a crowd surrounded them, staring in horrified fascination at the man who had been run down.

"I've got to go," she whispered. "I have to get out of here."

"You know you can't leave, Sweetheart. You have to wait for the police. They'll need us as witnesses." Nick came toward her, holding a hand out to her, his eyes dark with worry. She shook her head wildly, hearing the hysterical sob that ripped from her throat and knowing she was losing control.

Suspicion filled her mind and broke her heart as she studied the man she loved. Somewhere in her mind, she knew she was being irrational. She knew there was no real reason to suspect Nick, no reason for this mind-numbing terror that suddenly had her in its grip, but she remembered his sister telling her how crazy he was about her when they were teenagers.

150

She saw him in her mind's eye, holding up the burnt orange satin at Nina's, telling her it would look great on her.

"Stay away from me," she begged as he reached for her. "I know who you are."

"Jenny," he whispered, bewilderment flooding his eyes, "What are you talking about?"

"You. It's you," she heard her own voice as if from a distance. A roaring filled her ears as his arms came around her to keep her from falling.

Nick watched Jenny as she answered the policeman who was questioning her. They had already questioned everyone else, him included. The general consensus was that the vehicle was a dark sedan of some sort. That was the best description anyone had been able to give. No one had gotten a good look at the driver, but they all agreed they thought it was a man.

Jenny was pale and her turquoise eyes were huge in her face as she nodded her head.

He could just make out what the policeman was asking.

"They say you were the first one to get to him. Is that correct?"

She nodded.

"Did he say anything?"

"No," she said quickly, eyes darting toward Nick.

Nick raised his eyebrows, wondering about the frightened look on her face.

"Can you tell us anything that would help identify the driver?"

Jenny shook her head.

"Thank you, Ms. Lewis." He put his arm on her as she started back toward Nick. "By the way, do you have any idea why Officer Bowen was contacting you?"

"I don't know that he was," she answered softly.

Nick was surprised at her answer. They had both heard the man call out to her. He had said so to the police officer only moments ago.

"Ms. Lewis, both Mr. Jensen and Tommy Jackson say they heard Officer Bowen call your name. Are you saying you didn't hear him?"

"Yes, Officer. That is exactly what I'm saying."

"Thank you," the officer said, his eyes meeting Nick's questioningly.

Nick shrugged and looked toward Jenny as she bent to pick up Milton's leash.

"What was that all about?" He inquired when the officer was gone.

"What?" she asked, wide-eyed.

"Why did you lie to him?"

"Nick, I have to go home."

Angered welled up in him as she called for Milton and clipped the leash to his collar.

"Jenny, wait! You can't just walk away. Why did you lie to him?"

She looked straight at him, her eyes wide and bright, the fear and fury in them equally visible.

"I was protecting you," she said and Nick sucked in his breath.

"What?" he demanded. "Why?"

She looked at him, tears of fury filling her eyes.

"Because I love you," she cried and stalked away.

He stood staring after her. Questions drummed through his mind. What in the world was she talking about? Had she lost her mind? Protecting him from what? Then above it all, the quiet, desperate admission, *I love you.*

He was tempted to follow her, to demand that she tell him exactly what was going on. Instead, he turned toward his own house. She would tell him when she was ready.

Until then, he would leave her alone and let her sort things out. He knew it had been hard for her when Ellie died and witnessing this evening's accident hadn't helped.

# CHAPTER THIRTY TWO

Nick was the only person in the teachers' lounge late the next afternoon when the local news reported Neil Bowen's death.

"Officer Neil Bowen of the St. Johns County Police Department was killed near the historic district late yesterday in a hit and run accident. He had been a police officer for two years. If anyone has any information regarding the car or its driver, police ask that you call the number on the screen."

Nick started to change the channel but stopped when the newscasters eyes widened in surprise and she went on talking.

"In an apparently unrelated case, Officer Bowen's partner, Franklin Kelly, died yesterday when he was crushed by the vintage car he was restoring. Officer Kelly was a ten-year veteran of the police department. He and Officer Bowen had been partners for the last two years. Again, the police are saying the two deaths are unrelated."

Could their deaths really be unrelated? Could they be tied to Jenny?

He remembered the fear in her eyes when she had looked at him. He had thought she was suffering from shock after seeing Neil Bowen's death. Now, he realized the fear had been directed at him. But he couldn't understand why. Had Bowen said something to her before he died? How had she reached the conclusion that she should be afraid of him? And why in the world was she willing to protect him if she thought he was the one who wanted to kill her?

He cursed vehemently as he grabbed the remote and turned the television off. What did he do now? Wait for her to come to her senses and realize he would never hurt her?

Go to her house and demand she acknowledge he would never hurt her?

None of that was important compared to the fact that someone was trying to kill her. That overrode any wound to his pride or his heart. He had no idea what to do.

She was supposed to be with Sam today. He'd warned her to stay out of sight, but knowing the two of them, she was probably out parading through town pretty as you please.

Would she recognize the killer when she saw him? Could it have been someone she knew? In the last two weeks, she'd seen numerous people she knew, people she hadn't seen in six years. Was it mere coincidence that they showed up now, when the killer had resurfaced and the butterfly had reemerged?

He needed to talk to her, to confirm she was fine. He dialed her number, but there was no answer. After several more tries, he rushed toward his truck, telling the dean of boys he was leaving as they passed each other in the hall.

He reached her house in record time, and he cursed out loud when he found her car in the drive but no sign of her at all. He ran across the street, sure he'd find her there with Sam, but when he asked for Sam, his breath froze in his throat.

"I'm sorry, Nick," the proprietor said. "Officer Conway checked out this morning."

"What do you mean, 'checked out'?"

"He said he had to get back home. Something about a case he'd been working on." "Thanks!" he said, already pulling his phone out as he dashed to the car.

When the switchboard operator at the Brevard County Sheriff's Office answered, he quickly asked for Sam Conway.

"I'm sorry, sir, there's no one here by that name," the operator said in a clipped, no-nonsense voice.

"Listen," Nick said, "This is an emergency. Life or death. And I need to speak to Sam Conway. If he's not there, maybe you could find out how I could reach him."

"Sir, I am telling you, there isn't anyone here by that name."

"Fine, don't connect me to Sam Conway. Just connect me to any detective. This has to do with two officers who were killed in St. Augustine yesterday."

154

Instantly, the phone line filled with a radio station playing classic rock as he was put on hold.

"This is Lieutenant Mark Bentley," a gruff voice barked into the phone.

"Lieutenant Bentley, this is Nick Jensen. I desperately need to speak to Detective Sam Conway."

"Sam Conway, you say?" The man sounded genuinely confused.

With an exasperated sigh, Nick rubbed his forehead. He was getting a killer headache.

"Sam Conway. He's the officer assigned to protect Genevieve Lewiston."

"Mr. Jensen, at one time we had an officer named Sam Conway here, but he's been dead for fifteen years."

"You've got to be mistaken," Nick told him. "He's been here in St. Augustine for the last three weeks. She met him six years ago after her abduction."

"Genevieve Lewiston? That's the girl we found, right? The one with the butterfly? Model or something?"

"Yes, yes, that's right. And this detective, Sam Conway, he helped her after she got out of the hospital. He came here a few weeks ago and told her the guy had resurfaced, that he was tied to some other murders and he was after her. He was sent her to protect her."

The detective was silent for a long, drawn out moment.

"Mr. Jensen, we haven't attempted to contact Ms. Lewiston. We've been working with your local police, but any protection detail would come from them."

"Was the real Sam Conway involved in protecting Genevieve Lewiston six years ago?" Nick demanded.

"Mr. Jensen, I don't think you understand. This department had nothing at all to do with Genevieve Lewiston after we closed our investigation. We had no idea where she went or what she was doing. We saw no reason to protect her when we believed the attempt on her life was related to her work as a model. We have recently reopened our case based on new information, but like I said, our detectives have been working with your sheriff's office."

His stomach dropped.

"So who the hell is this guy?"

"Do you have any email address? I want to send you over a picture done by a sketch artist in Lake City."

"Of who?"

"I'm pretty sure it's the man you think is Sam Conway."

Nick gave him his email address and drove home at breakneck speed.

"He told her about the note."

"What note?"

"The note saying he was coming for her, that he would kill a girl a week if she didn't turn herself over to him. The note saying she needed to become the Butterfly Girl again."

"To my knowledge, there has never been any such note." He paused. "Mr. Jensen, where is Ms. Lewiston?"

"I don't know." He sat up straight in the seat. "Sam was supposed to look after her while I went to work. I'm home!"

Once inside, he pulled up the email and opened the attachment. Ice-cold fear ripped through him as he stared at the sketch.

"Is that the guy you know as Sam Conway?"

"Yes," Nick said hoarsely.

"Mr. Jensen, that man is Steven Hollis. His father-in-law was my partner, Sam Conway. Sam's daughter, Vanessa, died of cancer a couple years after she and Steve got married, and Sam died several years ago. He and Steve stayed close after Vanessa's death, and Sam thought of him as a son. He was always updating me on Steve just like he had updated me on Vanessa. A few months before his death, Sam told me he was worried about Steve. I don't know why. He didn't elaborate. Just said he was having some problems. I didn't ask, because I knew Sam. He'd tell me when he was ready, whether I wanted to hear it or not."

Through the phone, Nick heard the creak of Bentley's chair, the rip of paper and the clink of metal against glass. Coffee, Nick thought impatiently, looking down at his own cup, which had now gone cold. Another squeak of the chair and Bentley went on.

156

"I went to visit Steve after Sam died. Just to make sure he didn't need anything. I tell you, Jensen, it was one of the strangest experiences of my life. Steve led me into this room filled with dead butterflies. It was downright creepy having all those little dead creatures staring at me. And to top it off, he spent the whole time I was there sitting in this huge, ugly chair, twirling a butterfly with a six-inch needle through its body and telling me how many butterflies have women's names. I hate to admit it, but I left after only a few minutes. I thought the guy had gone nuts. It never occurred to me he was a serial killer."

"Mr. Jensen, you need to find Ms. Lewiston as soon as we possibly can. If he's gone to this much trouble, he must plan to take her. All of his murders have happened around the first of May. That means he could strike anytime now."

Nick was out the door, backing his car out of the driveway before Bentley finished talking.

He pulled to a stop in front of Jenny's house and ran up the drive. Maybe she just hadn't heard him earlier. Maybe she'd gone for a walk.

"Jenny!" he yelled as he knocked on the door. "Jenny!"

Derek Carson pulled up next door.

"Hey, Coach Jensen. If you're looking for Ms. Lewis, she's not there. I saw her downtown about an hour ago. She was walking down Cordova Street with that policeman
friend of hers."

"Thanks, Derek," he said. To Bentley, who was still on the phone, he said, "He's got her."

"My people are contacting the police there in town. Where are you?"

"I'm on my way to the historic district. Nina's Needle."

# CHAPTER THIRTY-THREE

"Thanks for coming with me, Sam. Talking to Nina always helps me see things more clearly." She bit into her sandwich and sighed with pleasure. "I love this place. They make the best Panini ever."

"You seem much more settled than you did this morning." He finished putting the lids on their sodas and pushed hers toward her before unwrapping his own sandwich. "Should we get her something to eat?"

"No, she said she's got leftover soup she's looking forward to eating. She prefers to eat at home. Says eating out is silly when she's got a perfectly good kitchen at home."

"A no nonsense kind of woman, huh?"

"Oh, yeah, that's Nina for sure" Except when it comes to sewing up orange silk blouses and turquoise ball gowns for a woman who never intends to wear them.

That impractical free spirit was nowhere in sight today, as Nina steadfastly refused to even entertain Jenny's suspicions about Nick.

"Genevieve," she had scolded when Jenny continued to try to get her to see, "that man would not hurt you. It is foolish to think he would. Go home, go to bed, everything will be better in the morning."

Then with a teasing twinkle in her eye, she added, "Better yet, find Nick Jensen, go to bed, and everything will be better before the morning."

Jenny had been so angry at Nina's lack of concern that the sexual innuendo had sent her blood boiling. She had stormed out of the shop without even saying good-bye.

"You really think Nick Jensen could be the killer?" Sam's voice interrupted her thoughts.

159

"Yes. No. I don't know what to think," she said, shaking her head in confusion before taking a huge gulp of the ice-cold drink. "But the policeman who was killed today said I knew him."

"You know a lot of people, Jenny. You know me, and you didn't automatically think of me. There must be some reason you thought of Jensen."

She laughed nervously, uncertainly.

"You're a cop. Of course it's not you. Besides, I've known you forever. If you wanted to kill me, I suppose you would have by now."

"Yeah, but Jensen's known you a while, too. Why would he be waiting?"

"I don't know. Why are you questioning me? Do you want me to suspect you?"

"Of course not," he said, too smoothly.

She tried to focus on his eyes, tried to see the emotion behind the words.

"Are you feeling alright?" Sam asked, covering her hand with his.

She peered at him through the strange fog that separated them, but the harder she tried to see him, the more ill and off balance she felt.

"No," she whispered, puzzled at the sudden onset of dizziness. "I don't know what's wrong with me."

"Come on. I'd better take you home."

Jenny pushed herself up from her seat but lost her balance and would have fallen if Sam's arms hadn't come around her.

"Sam?" Her voice was nothing more than a whisper.

He held her against his side tightly and half dragged her from the restaurant.

"Is she okay? Do you need some help?" The waitress asked through a long, echoing tunnel.

Jenny wanted to reassure her that she was all right but her head was too heavy to lift from Sam's shoulder and she couldn't force her mouth to move.

"She's fine," Sam said. "Just a little under the weather."

*It's more than that*, she thought as she tried to move her head. For a moment, it almost obeyed, but then dropped against Sam's arm.

"Come on, Sweetheart," he said as he helped her to his car. She fell onto the seat and he lifted her inexplicably useless legs and placed them inside.

She wondered frantically what was wrong with her. Had she had a stroke of some sort? Was this how it felt to die?

Shouldn't Sam be worried? Was he taking her to the hospital?

"I'm going to take care of you, Genevieve. You know I take exquisite care of my butterflies."

Chills swept through her as he spoke. She tried to force her hand to move toward the door handle, tried to speak, but it was a hopeless endeavor, and tears burned her eyes at her own helplessness.

"Don't be frightened. This stage is totally painless." His voice was calm and reassuring as he placed a hand on her head and gave it a gentle push to the right. "See how peaceful it looks? You'll love it there. I promise."

They crossed the Bridge of Lions and she saw the lights of the sailboats anchored in the Mantanzas River. They drove on and she knew they weren't going to the hospital.

After passing through a residential area, he pulled down a winding driveway that led to a secluded house overlooking the water. Trees formed a dense canopy in the backyard, effectively blocking the view from the other houses up and down the shore. She was going to die here, and there was no one to save her.

He lifted her effortlessly from the car and sat her up with her back to a tree overlooking the water. He knelt beside her, lifting her head with a gentle hand beneath her chin.

"It's a beautiful night. All the years we've lived here, I've loved this view. The moon on the water, the lights of the city. I have always found them so soothing. Something about those soft white lights against all that history makes it easier to live through the days between the butterflies. See how lovely it is? You couldn't ask for a better night."

He pressed his lips to her forehead.

161

"Where will you fly when you are free, Genevieve? Will you fly to the lights like a moth to the flame? Or will you fly to the warm beauty of a flower in the sunlight? Where will you go? What will you do?"

He stood to move to the car, and she felt herself slipping sideways toward the ground. Unable to stop the movement of her body, she fell to her side and lay there looking at the familiar lights of her beloved town.

The soft rustle of plastic sent terror rushing through her. *Oh, God, please not that, anything but that.*

"It's all right, Genevieve. I promise," he soothed as he lifted her in her arms and laid her down on the plastic. He crossed her arms over her chest and tied them together. She glimpsed the turquoise of the ribbon, the exact same color as the dress Nina made for her father's party. He pulled it so tightly against her skin, she felt her wrist snap and white-hot pain shot through her arm.

"Do you remember how it felt to be safe in your chrysalis, my beauty? Do you remember how free of pain you'll be?"

Tears streamed down her face, as lay there helplessly while he placed what she could only guess was a butterfly on her chest. She could feel the soft gossamer of its wings on the area of her chest that was left exposed by her shirt.

"This could have been over years ago. But maybe this is more fitting. Vanessa's been dead ten years. It took me a decade, but I did it. I fulfilled her wish. There are butterflies in heaven now."

Oh Nick, she thought, how could I have been so stupid?

She had to get away, to make it back to Nick and Nina and her parents. She needed more time.

"You were my favorite, Genevieve. You were always my favorite. And you were hers." He began to wrap the plastic around her legs and terror consumed her. "Vanessa adored you. She was beautiful, too. She had hair and eyes as black as midnight. And she wore your cosmetics. Every once in a while, I take out the gloss she wore on her lips. It smells like her, reminds me of her lips on mine. Tell her when you see her. Tell her I love her. Tell her I've done my best to play the game. Tell her I'll be there soon."

162

Jenny felt him stop twining the plastic. He was even with her hips and she could see his profile as he looked out across the river. Tears ran silently from his eyes as he stared at some distant point. He looked down at her again with a small, sad smile. His voice took on a faraway quality as he gave a soft recounting of what had driven him to the unspeakable act he was committing.

"Once more," he whispered brokenly as he took a small perfume bottle from his pocket and poured perfume into the hollow of her throat. "Just once more I want to smell her scent. I want to bury my face against a neck that still has the warmth of life pulsing through its veins and let the scent of her fill my senses."

The cold, fragrant liquid ran down her neck and into her hair, and with a sob, he buried his face against her neck. She could feel his tears following the trail of the perfume down her neck and dampening her hair.

How had he kept his insanity hidden so well? Why had he waited so long to do what he was doing now?

She tried to imagine herself as a butterfly, floating away from the place she lay, away from Sam Conway sobbing against her neck, and the heavily scented air filling her lungs. Where would she fly when she died? Would they find her soon? Or would her body lay here in Sam's yard, rotting inside her plastic cocoon until he was certain she had joined his wife in heaven? Could she stay here, flying above the city, the fort, the endearing tourist attraction or would she be forced to fly away?

With only a weak hold on reality, she forced her mind to calm, forced herself to focus. She couldn't control her body at this moment, but she refused to die a crazy woman.

After what seemed an eternity, Sam took a shuddering breath and moved away from her.

"I killed three girls before I got to you last time. Three beautiful girls; each of them had butterfly names, so it wasn't hard to find the kind they were. Then it was your turn. I knew whom I chose, but I had to work hard to find you. When I found you, I was thrilled. I knew Vanessa would be so happy to have you with her. When you escaped, I came to the hospital. I was going to kill you there like I did your friend, but I couldn't. It wasn't your time, and by the time it was, I had become rather attached to you. Maybe it was your eyes; you have unforgettable eyes, Genevieve. Did you know that's how your butterfly keeps safe? She has an eyespot on each wing. The eyes frighten predators away. I'm sure your eyes hold the same power. Well maybe they don't have the power to frighten, but to protect. I wasn't scared of you; I was simply powerless to harm you again. I thought maybe I could just let you go; maybe I could let you hide away and not be a butterfly. But I couldn't. There had to be one more butterfly. I had nine surrounding Vanessa's and there had to be one more to complete the circle. I knew it had to be you, the one who would mean the most to her. I couldn't just kill you as you were, though. I had to see you in all your glory once more, had to show Vanessa that you would never take her place in my heart. I always told her that she was my Butterfly Girl."

He secured the plastic around her head and face, leaving just an inch or so open as he continued to speak.

"By the way, Genevieve, I was really sorry I had to kill your friend. I actually did like her. But I wasn't sure what those officers told her, and I couldn't risk that she knew who I was. Her name didn't match a butterfly, but I think Vanessa will understand. Not everyone can be special, and Vanessa was too kindhearted to hold that against her."

He looked down at her. His face softened a little as he touched her cheek.

"I promise this won't hurt, Jenny. It won't seem like it takes any time at all." He smiled a rather sad, apologetic smile, "Good-bye, my friend."

*No, Sam, no! Please!* Jenny's mind cried out in panic as the plastic covered her face. She tried to force herself to breathe shallow, to use as little air as possible. She tried desperately to move her arms or feet, thinking if she could find a stick or rock, she could move back and forth against it until she put a hole in the plastic. But it was no use; she might as well have been completely boneless.

As Nick raced through the narrow streets of the oldest part of St. Augustine, Bentley explained how they'd come to connect the murders that had happened all over Florida for the past nine years.

It seemed a woman who was visiting her daughter in Jacksonville had been reading the newspaper and seen pictures of Jenny the night of her father's party. The woman had instantly thought the unnamed man in the picture looked familiar, but had been unable to put her finger on how she knew him. It was after reading the story, which went into detail about Jenny's past, and realizing some of the details were similar to a murder that had taken place near her home in Madison that she remembered where she'd seen him before.

She had been one of only a handful of people at a restaurant the night Steven Hollis and one of his victims, Sara Jones, had eaten there. Two days later, Sara was found dead near the state line. However, it wasn't until the woman read the article that she had connected the events. She and her daughter had gone to the Jacksonville police immediately.

Once they had knowledge of two cases with such similar circumstances, it hadn't taken the authorities long to connect the unsolved murders of nine women around the state. All of them were so similar, it was impossible not to think that the same person had committed them.

The victims themselves baffled the police, as they seemed to have nothing in common. They didn't have the same build, the same eye color, the same hair, the same lifestyle, nothing.

When Bentley was contacted with the news that the killer and one of his victims were living in St. Augustine, he had been shocked. When he had learned the suspect was Steven Hollis, he had been even more surprised.

However, when the signature of the killer had been brought to his attention, he had known instantly what they had in common.

Nick bounded from the car and dashed down the block. He burst into the shop and was greeted by the tiny old woman who informed him that Genevieve had left for home hours ago.

The police were there with seconds of his arrival and they began searching the surrounding neighborhood. They were just about to give up, when they stopped at a small sandwich shop a few blocks from Nina's store.

"I saw them. They were in a few hours ago," the waitress told them. "That poor lady got sick as a dog while they were here. He had to practically carry her out. If I were you, I'd check the hospital."

"We've got a house in Steve Hollis's name!" Nick glanced at the police officer who had been talking on his cell phone.

Nick was consumed with fear and panic as he followed the squad cars down the road that ran parallel to the Inlet. Bentley was still on the phone, warning him grimly that the girls were usually dead before they were found and that he should prepare himself for that possibility.

"Like hell I will," Nick growled, refusing to even think about it.

He couldn't bear the thought of losing her. She would be fine. Somehow, they would find her and she would be just fine. The thought became a litany in his head as the houses and trees rushed past and he searched for any sign of Jenny or Steven Hollis.

"We're here, he cried into the phone as he turned sharply into a rock-lined drive that led to the house. Nick jumped out of the car and rushed to the door of the large brick house.

As he pounded on the door and rattled the handle, the litany that Jenny was safe became a desperate prayer with each minute that passed.

Suddenly, a car raced from the back of the house and disappeared up the drive.

Nick tore around the side of the house as the cops yelled at him to wait and one of the cars took off after the fleeing vehicle.

"Jen!" he yelled, rushing headlong toward the river. In the moonlight, he could just make out the plastic-wrapped bundle lying there.

Her name ripped from his throat in an anguished roar as he ran toward her. He could see her huge blue-green eyes staring up at him through the plastic. They were too late, too late! His mind numb with fear, he tried to rip the plastic away from her with shaking hands.

166

One of the officers grabbed him, pulling him away from her while another cut the plastic away from her face and placed a hand to her neck.

"She's alive."

Tears of relief welled in Nick's eyes as the iron grip released him and he scrambled across the ground toward her.

"Thank God," he murmured as he gathered her limp body against him. "Thank God."

# CHAPTER THIRTY-FOUR

He stood on the Bridge of Lions looking at the lights of the boats anchored in the Bay. The fort glowed eerily against the darkened sky as he laid Vanessa's book on the parapet and climbed over the side of the bridge. Leaning back against the cool concrete, he carefully emptied the remaining pills into his hand. He could hear the sirens coming closer and closer. In a few minutes they would be here.

He had barely had her wrapped before he'd heard the car coming up the drive. He hadn't stopped to think. He'd just jumped in his car and sped away, leaving Genevieve lying there on the ground. They had found her too quickly. There was no way she was dead yet. He should have thrown her into the car. He wouldn't have gotten away, but by the time they caught him, she would have been dead. The circle would have been complete.

"I'm sorry, Vanessa." he murmured as he swallowed the pills.

He could run. They may never find him. But as he thought of leaving Florida, of hiding away for the rest of his life, away from the sun and the sea, away from all the things Vanessa had loved, he knew there was no way he could do it. He could never leave the memories behind.

He looked down at the dark, churning water. He would be able to tread water for only a moment or two before the medication did its job and he became paralyzed. Then, he would simply sink to the bottom. He had watched his butterflies die. It had always appeared to be an exceptionally painless thing to do. Dying couldn't possibly be more painful than living was. Death was only for a moment. Grief lasted a lifetime.

*He felt the initial effects of the medicine and, knowing his time was running out, he pictured himself as a huge butterfly; a black and orange Monarch with his wings stretched out in flight.*

*Vanessa! As he rushed toward the water, he saw her, the beautiful black butterfly with red bands across her wings. She rose toward him, hovering just above the surface, easing his fall and following him down as the cold, black water closed over his head.*

# EPILOGUE

Nick sat in the hospital waiting room impatiently waiting for the doctor to come through the doors at the end of the hall.

"I still can't believe you're marrying the Butterfly Girl," his brother, John, said from beside him.

Nick's eyes followed his to the place where Jenny leaned against the wall beside his mother. She was gorgeous in a soft pink sweater set and a straight black skirt, her arm in a sling to protect her broken wrist. He caught her eye and she smiled, as his heart welled with love and pride.

"Yeah, it is hard to believe, isn't it?" Nick said looking back toward John.

He sometimes couldn't believe it himself. Not that it mattered; he'd loved Jenny Lewis long before he had known she was the Butterfly Girl. And he loved her even more now that he had almost lost them both. He had decided as she sat there holding her on the bank of the river that he didn't care which one she was. He just wanted her to live. He wanted to love her for the rest of his life.

The doctor came through the doors, and the family rushed to meet him.

"It's a boy," he announced with a grin. "Mother and baby are doing fine. And, of course, Dad is doing more than fine. I'm sure he'll be out to boast in a few minutes."

As the doctor walked away, Nick wrapped his arm around Jenny from behind and pulled her back against him.

"I love you," he said in her ear.

"I love you, too," she answered as she leaned the back of her head against his chest.

"John can't believe I'm marrying the Butterfly Girl," he said, glancing over at his brother.

"You're not," she said, turning in his arms and looking into his eyes. "You're marrying me."

"What more could I ask for?" he murmured against her lips as he bent his head and kissed her thoroughly.

# About the Author

Gloria Davidson Marlow's heart is firmly planted in the northeast Florida neighborhood where she grew up in a family of commercial fishermen (and women!) Her home inspires her romantic suspense novels, allowing her to use beautiful settings from Amelia Island to St Augustine Beach in her books.

As she continues to write romantic suspense, she's a homemaker at heart who loves cooking, Florida wine, and making pickles and jellies. She plans to expand her horizons into learning crafts like soap and cheesemaking. She and her husband, also a commercial fisherman, have three very young grandsons with whom Gloria cannot spend nearly enough time.

For more of Gloria's books, visit her on the web at
http://www.gloriamarlowbooks.com/
Facebook: https://www.facebook.com/gloria.marlow